Sanctuary

Jan McDonald

Raven Crest Books

Copyright © 2017 Jan McDonald

The right of Jan McDonald to be identified as the author of this work has been asserted by her in accordance with the Copyright, Designs and Patents Act 1988

ISBN-13: 978-0-9934439-8-5

For Bill

SANCTUARY – Definition in Oxford English Dictionary – Refuge, or place of safety from pursuit or other danger..

CHAPTER ONE: BLOODY HERITAGE

High in Transylvania's Carpathian Mountains, Vasile Tepes sat in his favourite armchair contemplating the view from the massive picture window as the sun slipped behind the mountain; the mountain that fell away to the ancient castle ruins perched on the crags overlooking the Arges River at Poenari, and it was this view that drove and inspired him daily. As head of the House of Tepes, the ruins were once the fortress home of his great-grandfather Vlad III, more commonly known as Vlad the Impaler, or Vlad Dracula.

This was Vasile's sanctuary- *his* place- and this view was for no other eyes than his own and those of his most trusted servant, Nicolae. Tourists arrived at the ruins at Poenari daily to climb the hundreds of steps leading up to what was left of Dracula's fortress home, and Vasile longed for the day when all that would stop; when he restored the pile of stone once more to Castle Dracula.

The Dracula of fiction paled almost into insignificance next to the real Vlad, whose father, Vlad II, fought with every muscle, sinew and thought, against the invading Turks, determined to keep his homeland and his people safe, and in 1431 was invested with the Order of the Dragon, an organisation dedicated to fighting the Turkish invaders.

The dreadful name of Dracula was spawned from the old Romanian word *Dracul*, which means Dragon, and *Draculea* which means Son of the Dragon, an epithet that attached itself to Vlad at his birth, though in later years it became simply – *Dracula*. If fate is dictated by name, the word Dracul in Romanian also translates as Devil – so Dracula, Son of the Dragon, was also known as Dracula,

1

Son of the Devil.

As children, Vlad and his younger brother, Radu, were taken hostage by the Turks in an effort to bring his father to heel, during which time – years in fact – Radu changed his allegiance to the Turks and Vlad's anger and hatred were honed to the razor-sharp perfection of a Toledo steel blade. He emerged from captivity, a ruthless, blood-thirsty leader of his people who eventually regained the throne of Wallachia for the House of Tepes: Prince Vlad of Wallachia. Exactly when his taste for blood became literal no-one knows, but from him the ancient vampire lineage of the Born continued and continues.

Thoughts such as these were constant in Vasile's mind. Exquisitely aware of his heritage and his responsibilities, he was consumed with hatred for the Created – vampires that had been turned by another – and, as he watched throughout the centuries, he witnessed his ancestral home become nothing more than a pile of stone to be trampled underfoot by gawping tourists and vowed that one day the House of Tepes would rise again and that he would be the one to restore it, however long and whatever it would take.

His disdain for the Vampire High Council and their codes and ethics were another thorn in his side, as were some of its officials. Mihai Rabinescu – Michael Rabb to the human world - was the Patriarch of the Council. He was as incorruptible as he was stubborn and his fierce defence of the Created was an abomination to Vasile.

After the debacle in Greece - when his brothers Luca and Mircea were killed at the hands of Mihai, Beckett and Lane Dearing – Vasile had retreated to his lair in the Carpathians in a savage and incandescent rage against them all. There would be another war; the Created were an abomination, and they were multiplying nightly as they became hungry, vicious and reckless. They had to be wiped out and there was nothing the Council could do to stop it.

An alliance with the Greek vampire House of Vasilakis would be prudent. They were weak after the death of

Drakos, the head of their house, at those same hands that took his kin in Greece. There was a price to pay and he, Vasile Tepes, would exact the highest fee. The House of Vasilakis would serve his purpose; swelling his ranks, adding strength with their numbers and, in their weakened state, they would be easy to manipulate. After the war they would either be assimilated into the House of Tepes or they would perish; he didn't much care which.

His thoughts were interrupted by his awareness of the approach of his servant Nicolae. His raised his head in anticipation.

"Sir, your visitors have begun to arrive. Alexis Vasilakis bids you thanks for your invitation. He has arrived with four others of his house. Georgios Popescu is also here with two of his brothers. They bring news of the Born in the United Kingdom, who regret their absence but pledge their allegiance."

Vasile allowed himself a small, satisfied smile. The Born were gathering; his time had come.

He dismissed his servant with a brief nod and strode to the huge window with its view of the ruins of Castle Dracula on the crags above the Arges River; the same crags and river that had claimed the life of his great-grandmother, Vlad's first wife, over six centuries ago, when she flung herself from the castle, over the jagged rocks and into the Arges River below, rather than be captured by the Turks.

"You will rise again Vlad. Our house will once again give birth to terror in our enemies. I have kept your secret all these centuries and I am close to finding that which will give you life again; your chalice will give you life, my ancestor, and the House of Tepes will be great once more."

He turned abruptly and went to greet his guests.

They were waiting for him in the great hall, built and decorated in true gothic style with a huge baronial fireplace, ablaze and dominating one wall. Several couches and massive armchairs were scattered throughout the hall and Vasile's guests had been made welcome. Sumptuous tapestries and ancient portraits adorned the walls of stone; stone that had been hacked from the very bedrock of the mountain.

Vasile's presence was immediately felt, ending all conversation abruptly. Every head was turned towards him in a cocktail of curiosity and apprehension. To all, the invitation had felt more like a command. Alexis Vasilakis had taken the greatest exception to it and had wasted no time in sharing his opinions but – even he – had not been able to stay away.

Vasile bowed theatrically to the assembly of vampires of the Born. "The House of Tepes bids you welcome, friends. I am honoured to receive you and I trust you have been made comfortable." It was a statement rather than an enquiry.

He moved into the middle of the company, the better to address them all. Vasile was almost beyond handsome, his shining ebony hair, that would never fade to grey, hung to his neck and draped his shoulders. His looks would have forgiven him adopting the exquisite, if ancient, clothing but he chose instead to prefer fashionable and finely tailored suits from Paris and London. His long, aquiline nose and dark, arched eyebrows replicated those of his great-grandfather and, should he decide to grow a moustache, the resemblance would be exact. The same cruel lips parted, giving a brief glint of sharp, long, white teeth in the candlelight.

CHAPTER TWO: LINWOOD HOUSE

Friendship between a demon hunter and a vampire is as unlikely as an alliance between Van Helsing and Dracula but, the bond that had grown between Mike Travis and Father Paul Beckett - Beckett to everyone - proved that anything was possible.

Mike's story had begun as an RAF helicopter pilot shot down in Afghanistan, where he clinically died in the crash, but was brought back by the skills of the military medics – the only thing was, he had returned with a new ability; he could see ghosts and communicate with them. In an effort to try to understand this new phenomenon he became an avid investigator of the paranormal realm. As with all things, one investigation led to another, one spirit to another until finally – and perhaps inevitably – he found himself hunting and doing battle with high-ranking demons. Sometimes winning, sometimes not. Often not.

Unsurprisingly, delayed onset of Post-Traumatic Stress Disorder hit him hard. Enter Beckett.

Father Paul Beckett – ex-Catholic priest-turned psychologist and psychotherapist-turned vampire – had issues. Of course he did, with that history. Back when his life was less complicated, as a Catholic priest in a relatively small parish, his sister Grace died horribly at the hands of a vampire and, what was worse, she rose again in the hours of darkness. Only the arrival of the beautiful and ancient vampire, Lane Dearing, saved his sanity that night. And it was on that night that he lost his faith; there could be no God, for no God would create such things and allow them to live and destroy. But they did.

He walked away from everything that night, stepping into years of study that had qualified him in Psychology and Psychotherapy – 'heal thyself' had been his mantra. It hadn't worked.

So he turned his attention to others – and then it happened. One of his patients, Katerini Pappas, started showing alarming tendencies that Beckett had seen before. Little things to start with, but then crazy things; crazy things that he thought were works of fevered imaginations. Until he accepted the truth: that vampires exist and they are out there. He had failed to help Grace, and not only did he repeat his failure with Katerini but he became a blood-drinker himself after his efforts to save her ended with him being bitten, fed on, and turned, by the very one he tried to save. Only vengeance was left to him then.

He learned much as a vampire: that there was the possibility of God's existence, although the jury did sometimes appear to be out on that; that revenge wasn't the answer - justice was; and that praying over a departing soul, good, bad or evil, would help that soul to find peace. Some would say they didn't deserve it – Beckett was still waiting for a sign. In the meantime, he served as priest to the vampire community and worked alongside Lane Dearing as a partner in her psychiatric practice. Of course Beckett had issues.

Enter Mike Travis.

And so their friendship grew in depth and quality as each helped the other find some kind of understanding. Now Mike's wife, Beth, was ill – Beckett's kind of ill.

"Tell me if I'm imagining it, Beckett. There's something, a subtle something that I can only describe as 'her', my Beth. Just a glimmer, but it's there. She's there."

Beckett's smile reached his storm-grey eyes, a rare occurrence these days. "I think there's every sign that we are getting somewhere. But, Mike … don't let's get ahead of ourselves … this is going to take a very long time. Yes, I agree, there is a subtle change, and that's what we've been waiting for. But it's way too early to expect full recovery and any attempt to push it would be disastrous … and we have to face the extreme possibility that we may never get her back." He didn't want to encourage false expectations in his friend, but honesty had always been something that was taken for granted between them. He smiled again, "I think we're getting somewhere – slowly, but we're getting there."

They were sitting in a large bay window overlooking the immaculately-manicured lawns of Linwood House, the headquarters of The Strazca, in the Cotswolds as the sun went down. They had left Beth in her room, still blissfully at peace in her own world; a world of retreat and isolation where no demons existed and Hell wasn't on the map.

Mike nodded. "How about you, Beckett?"

"Busy. When I'm not seeing patients, I'm at the Sanctuary."

Mike didn't miss the hint of wistfulness in the word 'Sanctuary'. He had heard it mentioned between Beckett and his young assistant, Darius, on several occasions though he had never asked about it. He wasn't sure he wanted to know but, sitting there opposite Beckett, - who was casual in his jeans and open-necked shirt, looking ever-leaner - Mike could see the sadness behind the squall in his eyes.

"The Sanctuary?" he queried, and then, in an effort to make light of his ignorance, "Have you been clubbing, Beckett?"

That brought an involuntary laugh from Beckett. "You're good for me, Mike. Sorry, I thought you knew about the Sanctuary." He paused. "Does that mean they don't know about it here? That's hard to believe." The degree of difficulty in belief was apparent on his face.

"If they do, I haven't come across it. Yet. At least I don't think so. Tell me."

Beckett appeared to be contemplating something for several minutes before he said, "OK, come on, there's nothing more to do for Beth today. Come with me, I'll show you."

7

Mike considered briefly finding Roman Woolfe – he was Beth's benefactor, the owner of Linwood House and the head of a secret organisation known (to those that did know) as The Strazca. Mike thought about telling Roman where he was going, but his instincts told him that he would get a fuller explanation if he went as a friend and not in any official capacity. Beckett trusted Mike with his life, and vice versa; now was not the time to give any cause for doubt. Before bringing this home to Roman Woolfe, first Mike would get permission from Beckett. There were lines within friendship that you didn't cross.

They passed the first part of the journey to Newport in intermittent bursts of amiable conversation, until Mike could hold off no longer.

"So, what is it, then? This *Sanctuary*. Sure it's not a nightclub?" he teased.

Beckett didn't look away from the road in front. "I'd rather show you, Mike. We're almost there. Think about the meaning of the word 'sanctuary'. It is a place of refuge, a place of safety, for anyone in danger from anything. My world isn't pretty, Mike. Some of the worst of our kind are the worst of your imagination. They feed, they injure, they kill, and, sometimes they turn their prey. And then they leave them; lost, alone and with a ravening hunger that can be sated in only one way, a thirst that can only be quenched by one thing. And so it goes on, a never-ending cycle. More beget more.

"We have codes of ethics, Mike; codes that protect newly-turned vampires – and that's where the Sanctuary comes in. You'll see."

Mike had to settle for that; he wasn't in a hurry.

CHAPTER THREE: TRIP OF A LIFETIME

Lucy Eastman checked everything for the eighth time. Passports – check, flight tickets – check, joining instructions – check, though she knew them off by heart; Heathrow Airport, seven-thirty in the gallery opposite the TAROM check-in desk. There were eight in their party plus the tour guide and she had gained the impression, whilst paying for the tickets in an online auction, that the remainder of the group already knew each other, but it didn't bother her. Everything was too exciting to think about details.

She hadn't been able to believe her luck when her bid won the auction for the trip. She hadn't wanted to spend as much as she'd eventually bid on them, but she'd been carried away with last-minute auction-frenzy. Still, it would be worth it, the trip of a lifetime; a Dracula Tour of Romania, taking in the sights, sounds and romance of Dracula's homeland, visiting castles and dungeons and 'living' the Dracula fantasy in the footsteps of Bram Stoker's Jonathan Harker.

Chalk and cheese could only describe Lucy and her partner, Dan. He was a science teacher – serious, intellectual and he believed only in what could be proven as well as seen. Folklore and empirical evidence were anathema to him, although he indulged Lucy's obsession with vampires and all things gothic to the point of allowing her several shelves in his bookcase but, this trip was almost a stretch too far. He had agreed to it on the condition that he wasn't going to dress up as the Victorian gothic and play, in his words, 'silly buggers'.

Already lost in a whirlwind of images, she accepted the

9

condition with a grin. They had foregone a wedding and exotic honeymoon in favour of a deposit for their small portion of suburbia and, now, two years later they deserved a break. "Something different," Lucy had said, "something – oh, I don't know – something adventurous!"

Immediate visions of safaris or hiking holidays through some obscure mountain region had created havoc in his head, so when she found the trip on the on-line auction site, it had been somewhat of a relief. Lucy would spend two weeks soaking up the atmosphere and the tourist set-ups, treading in the footsteps of the doomed Jonathan Harker of Bram Stoker's imagination, playing vampire in the evenings with her impressive array of gothic gowns which were all her own handiwork, while he soaked up the culture, the *real* culture, in the *real* world, and maybe took in a historic site or two. After all, two weeks would go quickly and perhaps it would be enough to overcome her obsession; all played-out.

At seven-fifteen and a few seconds, Lucy and Dan approached the appointed meeting place. A 'Gathering of Goths' was noticeable by its absence. Dan frowned, he was already feeling the wriggle of a tiny maggot of doubt about the whole thing but, his thoughts had no time to go anywhere as Lucy nudged him hard in the ribs. He exhaled loudly and bent forwards.

"Look, I think they're coming over here."

Dan looked up. Of course they were coming over there. A couple were sauntering towards them – long black coats, heavy black eye-liner, black jeans, pretty much black everything. His wriggling maggot morphed into a blow-fly. He pictured himself the odd-one-out of the party, an outsider, not party to their in-jokes and references. Maybe he should have watched one or two of Lucy's vast collection of vampire movies, well … maybe one. This was a mistake.

Lucy had refrained from the gothic look, as worn by the approaching couple, for two reasons. First, her restraint in that department had made Dan relax a little, and, second, she hadn't known what to expect; full-on Goth or a variety of tastes on display. She wished she hadn't refrained.

She smiled at the girl clomping towards her in boots that would survive the apocalypse. Had she caught her eye? No … maybe … yes … no. But that was OK, Goths weren't supposed to smile, were they? She allowed herself a nervous glance over at Dan and quickly looked away when she saw his expression. Well, he would get used to it and she was going to fulfil her dream.

Lucy's thoughts were in a tumble. Should they say hello first and introduce themselves? Or should they wait for the others to speak first. Say hello, yes; that was the best thing. But perhaps …

The girl leaned into her darkling partner and whispered something in his ear. He looked at them directly and said in his most menacing tone, laced with a Brummie accent, "Who are you bloody staring at?" This, muttered as they walked right on past, towards the exit.

Dan visibly relaxed and Lucy descended into a fit of giggling. She'd determined to have fun and it had started already.

"Hi. First to arrive?"

They spun around, surprised at the cultured voice from behind them.

The man looked to be in his early thirties and his well-manicured, outstretched hand erased the frown-lines from Dan's brow.

"Hi," the man said again, "Christian Iliescu, I'm your guide for the trip."

Dan took the proffered hand. "Dan," he said. "And this is Lucy, my partner. I'm afraid I'm not used to all this, Lucy is the one into all things fanged." His relief was obvious.

"Dan Jarvis and Lucy Eastman," Christian said, as he ticked their names off the list on his clip-board. "A culture vulture, is it? You won't be disappointed, Dan. There is history and culture in spades in Transylvania. You'll love it." Dan noted a tiny hint of Eastern European in the professional, English speech. Christian continued, "I think you're a pretty mixed bunch on this trip. It's a small group as you know; a lot smaller than usual in fact but it's the last tour of the season, so we ran it anyway."

Lucy raised a questioning brow, "The season? I didn't know there was a season for the tour."

Christian smiled; a genuine one that came from behind the professional lip movement. "Just over two weeks from now, the snow will fall and the Borgo Pass, along with the main highway through the Carpathians, will be closed. If, like last year, the snow lies as heavily in the rest of the region, villages and towns will be cut off. For weeks."

A moment of panic spread across Lucy's face. "What if the snow comes early?"

Christian laughed. "Don't worry, there are early warning signs of that. The people of the Carpathians know these things by instinct and they are saying three weeks yet, at least. You'll be home well before the first flakes fall over the highest peaks and the wolves come down from the forest."

There was something comforting in his voice; it had a deep, hypnotic quality that resonated on a different frequency, and yet Lucy had the fleeting feeling that he was making fun of her. She didn't know if she liked it. Then, all was normal again.

"That's a relief then," she laughed. "Are the rest of the eight all couples?"

Christian scanned his list, even though he must have it memorised; it was a short list. "No. There are two other couples and two single ladies. That's always awkward for the Masquerade Ball," he said, in a mock-confidential tone.

His mention of the Masquerade Ball was enough to calm any anxieties Lucy still had. She pictured it: a castle hotel high on the mountain, driven there by horse-drawn carriages through the pass that was flanked by dense forest, to alight in her black satin ball-gown at the foot of the huge flight of stone steps leading into the castle hall and ballroom. Then her reality-check kicked in. They were a party of eight; hardly enough for a ball in anyone's book. She would probably be wise to dial down her expectations.

But, just for a minute, she allowed her fantasy.

The rest of the group were, indeed, a mixture. The first thing Dan noticed was that he and Lucy were the oldest in the group – the rest being in their early twenties to his thirty-nine and Lucy's thirty-one. As Lucy suspected, the others did know each other and it soon became apparent that they had taken the place of another couple from the group, one of whom had been unexpectedly posted abroad by his department at the Foreign Office. The Goths were indeed interesting people; interesting people from varied backgrounds, all with one thing in common, a love of Goth and metal music and culture, tempered with a sense of fun and an encyclopaedic knowledge of every vampire movie to hit the big and not-so-big screens. Black eye-liner was in evidence but their mode of dress was fairly eclectic, from serious hippy, to jeans and t-shirt and back via the gothic romantic. Dan allowed himself to relax even further. This wasn't going to be so bad.

Introductions over, the group was herded towards the departure lounge to await their flight to Bucharest; Christian having already collected their passports and tickets and checked them in as a group, all they had to do was check in their luggage.

Dan and Lucy's travelling companions included a teacher, a solicitor, a nurse, a conservationist (that would be the hippy), a writer looking for a story and a bank clerk. Most of them were on the trip for the Dracula experience but it was the writer that declared the cultural passion. His name was Trevor, and he and Dan hit it off immediately.

As they had been checked in as a group, they were sitting close together during the flight, where ice was broken and measures taken, with a consensus at the end of it that they would all get along well and enjoy the trip to the max.

Conversation during the three-hour flight centred around different locations on their itinerary: Bistrita, where, in the footsteps of Jonathan Harker, they would stay at the present-day version of the Golden Crown Hotel and dine on robber steak – chunks of bacon, onion and beef, seasoned with pepper, strung onto skewers and roasted over an open fire in the traditional way; Sighisoara, the birthplace of Vlad Dracula; the ruins of the real Castle Dracula at Poenari with its fourteen-hundred-odd steps to the summit of the peak where the ruins squatted like some long-forgotten, skeletal monster.

Bram Stoker's book was nowhere to be seen; they knew it by heart. Dan made a mental note to acquire a copy. If he was going to be able to converse with his fellow travellers it would seem that this was essential, so while they were waiting to claim their luggage, he approached Christian when the others were in discussion about recent film adaptations of the immortal story.

"Christian, this is perhaps a little embarrassing. You see, I've never actually read the damn book and, if I am going to get out alive, I guess I should."

Christian grinned. "There's one on every trip; you're in good company. I learned early on in the job to keep a couple of copies in my case, you can have it as soon as it comes down the conveyor belt. Excuse me a minute – announcement time." He moved towards the group and spoke in his best tour guide voice.

"OK everyone, can I have your attention for a minute or two? Our luggage will be here imminently, and our small but comfortable coach is waiting for us outside. We begin our tour in Tirgoviste, the former capital of Wallachia. It is here that you'll be able to see and climb the famous Sunset Tower, otherwise known as the Chindia Tower, at the foot of which Vlad Tepes III, or Vlad the

Impaler, impaled his enemies. From there we go to Poenari – where, perched on top of a mountain, is the real Castle Dracula – for those of you who are fit there are fourteen hundred and eighty steps to be climbed! The citadel was probably built in the 14th century by the first Wallachian princes. Later on, it was modified and extended by Vlad the Impaler, whom you probably know better and more fondly as Dracula. In addition to all the stories and legends, the site offers great panoramic views of the mountains on both sides. Once you are at the top of the mountain, Transylvania welcomes you and we will reach the city of Sibiu in time for dinner. Ah, our luggage, I think."

Half an hour later, they were handing their cases to an amiable Romanian driver who tossed them carelessly into the luggage compartment of the coach. Christian handed a dog-eared, well-read, copy of Dracula to Dan with a smile. There was one traveller who would be occupied during the journey; he hoped the rest would be as easy.

Dan settled quickly into becoming absorbed by Bram Stoker's immortal words in his immortal book ....

CHAPTER 1

'.... *3 May. Bistritz. Left Munich at 8:35 P.M, on 1st May, arriving at Vienna early next morning; should have arrived at 6:46, but train was an hour late. Buda-Pesth seems a wonderful place, from the glimpse which I got of it from the train and the little I could walk through the streets. I feared to go very far from the station, as we had arrived late and would start as near the correct time as possible.*

The impression I had was that we were leaving the West and entering the East; the most western of splendid bridges over the Danube, which is here of noble width and depth, took us among the traditions of Turkish rule...'

CHAPTER FOUR: THE SANCTUARY

The seedy side of Newport's night-life was teeming with night-clubbers in varying degrees of intoxication – ranging from happy drunk, to loud and obnoxious, to leaning towards being arrested. This city's darkest haunts were like any other – except that this city had been the territory of a predatory and powerful vampire. That much Beckett had already hinted at.

Mike was alert as Beckett drove towards the docks, away from the neon-lit, new town-centre. He parked in front of an Indian restaurant, half-way between the town and the docks, in a dark back street.

"We're here," Becket said.

Mike looked around. "Either you're hungry or that's a front for something else."

"Tick, VG. I hope it isn't that obvious to anyone else."

Mike shook his head. "No, I'm *looking* for something else, and I've learned not to accept anything on appearance. Suspicion is my friend. Sadly. So, what is it? Curry, or something else?"

"Definitely something else. Before we go in, I'll give you a summary. I told you that we have codes of conduct and ethics designed to protect both humans and vampires alike. There are alternative ways to gain our nourishment without killing, maiming or … worse … turning. Centuries ago there was a war between the Born – the name speaks for itself – and the Created; – those turned into a vampire. It was then that the Vampire High Council was formed – to police our own so that vampires could live among the humans without causing, or being, hurt. As in all societies, there is the elite and vampires are no different; there is a growing element of the Born that reject our ethics and see

17

humans only as a food source to be disposed of after use. The Created also have their bad guys who also reject the Council and our laws.

"Most often, the victims are left to die, discarded as so much packaging, but sometimes a victim is turned and, when that happens, the sire has a responsibility to the infant vampire, just as any parent to a child. Those who reject the Council and the vampire codes are beginning to turn their victims and abandon them to their fate. The turning is an exquisite agony that cannot be described, and then comes the thirst and the hunger – the desperate need to feed that overtakes every other instinct, even the killer instinct."

"I'm beginning to get the picture. Jesus, Beckett, I thought demons were a hard enough concept. I clearly haven't been doing this job long enough."

Beckett continued, "So, we have volunteers who discreetly hang around the usual places and, if they find a newly-turned alone and suffering, they bring them here – to the Sanctuary. Come on, I'll show you."

"Did you do this?" Mike asked.

A shadow fell across Beckett's eyes. "No. Someone very dear to me created this. She is a brilliant doctor and psychiatrist, a vampire, and over four-hundred years old. And I thought I was going to lose her. I still might."

Mike let it go, mainly because he didn't know what to say and Beckett's face was now a mask of stone.

Inside the front door, the entrance to the Indian restaurant was on the left and a solid door with a swipe-card lock and a keypad stood directly ahead. Beckett swiped his card and tapped on the keypad. A buzzer sounded followed by a clunk as the door yielded to them.

Mike let out a low whistle as he scanned the interior. It was like a hotel reception, manned by a Goth girl in her early twenties with her head bent over her phone. Her desk was central in the room which acted like a hub with corridors leading in the four cardinal directions, and behind the reception desk a wide flight of stairs led to the upper floor.

"It goes way back behind the restaurant and the upstairs covers the entire footprint of the building. There are bedrooms, clinics, feeding rooms and even an operating theatre. The whole place is sound-proofed and enclosed in carbon filters."

"Hence the absence of a vindaloo aroma!" Mike laughed.

Beckett allowed himself a brief flicker of a smile that he really didn't feel. He approached the girl on the reception desk.

"Hello Sadie, everything seems quiet. Anything happening?"

Sadie looked up from her phone and smiled at Beckett. "Hi Beckett, yes, a quiet one for a Friday. A young lad was brought in about an hour ago, still in the last phase of the turning and a donor is on the way."

Mike's eyes were wide as he followed Beckett. "Donors? Really?"

Beckett's expression was still flat. "Yes. They are mostly recruited from medical students and some victims are lucky enough to have a family member or loved one as a donor. Other than that we have a network which includes most every part of society; doctors, undertakers, lawyers, you name it. Some of our doctors work in teaching hospitals and they can tell if a student can handle the truth of our existence and then be willing to help – and more importantly - keep silent. The donors are handsomely paid I assure you. They are only allowed to donate at regular intervals unless we have an emergency. Most vampires feed from plastic bags, Mike, not veins. But, as I said, there are those that … well, let's say, make this place necessary. There are other places like this in many cities around the world, but this one is Lane's baby. The whole idea was hers and this was the first of them. The Mothership, if you like."

Beckett opened a door at the end of the corridor and pushed it wide for Mike to enter. He felt as if he had stepped back in time. It was a beautiful room, dressed with fine art of every description, antique furniture and adornments. In the middle of the vast Persian carpet, between two elegant but comfortable sofas, there was a beautiful, antique table with a crystal decanter filled with whisky and matching glasses on a solid silver tray. Mike sensed that it was extremely old just by looking at it. He was puzzled.

"This is a far cry from your sitting room at the Cedars," he said, referring to Beckett's home and practice just outside Abergavenny.

Beckett smiled. "This is Lane's room. Most of this was her stuff from when she was human – before her turning. She was beyond wealthy back then, but even so, if you live for four hundred years trying to keep a low profile and you're clever, it's easy to amass great wealth. Lane uses a bare minimum of hers for her own comfort and the rest is put to good use. Our lawyers handle everything for her, leaving her free to do what she does best – helping the vampire community by holding a high rank on the Council, running this place and also her regular psychiatric practice."

Mike looked around appreciatively and sat on the sofa opposite Beckett, while his friend poured two glasses of the old, single malt.

Beckett took a swallow of the scotch. "She's still in the Long Sleep, healing – it's been five years now, since she was mauled close to death," he said, referring to the deep vampire sleep that could last from decades to a century. "That bastard Vasile Tepes will pay when I can get my hands on him, but he's back in his lair in the Carpathians, too well-protected to get to. But when he sets foot away from there and I hear about it, I will be waiting for him."

"It was him that almost did for her?" Mike asked.

Beckett nodded.

20

Mike took a drink. "We have a lot in common, Beckett. Someone you love was damaged by something evil. Now you hunt it. We're not so very different."

"I guess not. So, are we going to continue drinking and getting more and more maudlin, or shall I show you around?"

Mike grinned and tossed the remains of the whisky down his throat. "Come on. I'm impressed so far, and prepared to be dazzled."

They stood up with a new understanding; their bond strengthened.

"I'll show you the clinics and rest areas upstairs," Beckett said, as they walked back towards the hub.

Half-way up the stairs, Beckett stopped abruptly and bent forwards, clasping his chest. He staggered sideways before Mike could grab him, sucking in deep gulps of air that went nowhere, leaving him breathless. And then it was over as quickly as it had begun. Beckett was even paler than usual.

"I heard her, Mike. I heard her call my name. And I felt her. I felt her pain. Lane."

"What the hell …?" Mike gasped, as he lifted Beckett upright.

"Something happened. Something …" He didn't finish, he leaned back against the wall and grabbed his phone from his pocket, staring at it. It rang.

"How do you *do* that?" Mike asked.

Beckett ignored him. "Anna, is she …?" he said into the phone.

Sister Anna, a nun in Greece who watched over and took care of Lane in her vampire sleep, answered him briefly.

"She still sleeps, but there is a change. You told me to notify you immediately of any change."

"What change?" Beckett demanded.

"Lane still sleeps, but she is moving occasionally. It began this morning, only subtle at first, but a moment ago she moved her hand." There was a brief hesitation in her voice. "And there is something else ... I believe that someone is watching me."

"I'm on my way..." Beckett disconnected the call.

Mike raised an eye-brow. "Is everything OK?"

"No. I have to go. I'll call Darius to come and pick you up and give you a lift back and he needs to take care of this place while I'm away. I think Lane is waking up – it could be days, or weeks until she's fully awake. When she went to sleep I promised her that I would be there when she woke up. I intend to keep that promise. And Anna says someone is watching her. While Lane sleeps, her location is safe from the likes of Vasile Tepes: when she wakes , the ancients will be able to locate her. She won't be safe."

Mike frowned. "Who is Vasile Tepes?"

"One of the most cruel, most ruthless vampires to walk this earth and who, one day, I intend to kill."

CHAPTER FIVE: LOST CHALICE

The meeting of The Born from the great vampire houses went on into the dark Carpathian night. All were agreed: the Created were out of control, an infestation that had to be culled, even though the problem had begun close to home many centuries ago. The first of the Created had to have been spawned from one of their own and from there the progression had gone on unchecked.

Most of the Created adhered to the despised codes and laws of the Council but there were others, the dark ones, who revelled in their blood-power and mistakenly believed that their status was enhanced by turning their prey. Drunk on blood and power, they ravaged the underbelly of society – for that is where their prey would go unmissed and unmourned.

Once a vampire is established in their new world, the need to drink for survival comes at lengthier intervals and they can live alongside humans without detection. But there was a new breed among the Created – angry, disrespectful, violent, and with no regard for the ancient ones – who hunted and fed in an orgy of bloodlust just because they could. They were a danger to all vampires, as sooner or later they would be unmasked and the human population – their food – would not be such easy prey. If there was one thing that could be said of humans, it was that they were inventive. They would find ways to kill the vampires – Born and Created alike.

If they were to survive, another vampire war was inevitable and, to this end, an alliance between the two houses of Tepes and Vasilakis would be beneficial to all. So said Vasile Tepes to the gathering.

Opposition from the House of Vasilakis was muted,

much to the surprise of Vasile and the others of the Tepes clan, and it was left to Alexis Vasilakis to speak for them, although the air was thick with mistrust.

"Fine words, Vasile, but who is to be head of this alliance? You, no doubt! My House will not be subservient to the House of Tepes. Never! The history of your House proves only that it serves its own interests with ruthless disdain and, delivers its own justice on any who oppose it."

There was a murmuring of agreement amongst the others as Alexis continued, "And what of our territories? Do they also become the property of the Tepes dynasty?"

Vasile Tepes raised a hand. "Have a care, Alexis, that you do not take advantage of my hospitality. I have said an alliance and, an alliance is what I mean – equality in every respect. If we continue to oppose each other, extinction of the Created becomes so much more difficult. Come, we are agreed on that course of action – why then, do you balk at a solution? I have no desire for your territory, my friend. And as for the history of our Houses, I see you make reference to my great-grandfather, Vlad – I would urge you to look to your own lineage. It paints no fine picture. If we continue in this manner, the war will be between ourselves while the abomination that is the Created continues to thrive. How can that be tolerated? I can see there is much that has been said which needs discussion, therefore I am ending this meeting with an open invitation to enjoy my hospitality before you all leave to consider my proposals."

His eyes darkened as they fixed on Alexis Vasilakis. He hoped it wouldn't come to it, but any rejection of an alliance would be met with immediate and ruthless aggression. Once the House of Vasilakis was brought to heel, the rest would follow; the name of Tepes was still feared among the vampire race. Alexis had got that part right. And he knew it.

"My House thanks you for your hospitality, Vasile, and I am certain I speak for the rest of the gathering when I say that we will consider your proposals. For the House of Vasilakis, I thank you for your continued generosity, but we wish to leave now to consult all members of our House."

This effectively brought the gathering to a close and, one by one, the Houses took their leave. Vasile was enraged; it hadn't gone according to his plan and that was always a precursor to someone not having a good day. The resurrection of his ancestor was becoming more urgent. He, Vasile, had led the House of Tepes for centuries but, even in his supreme arrogance, he knew that it was Vlad that would unite the Born. His terrible name would be enough.

But, to do that, he needed the lost chalice.

Every folk tale holds a grain of truth and this was no exception. Vlad III – Vlad Dracula – held an iron grip on his people through a reign of terror and enforcement of order that none dared oppose when the legend of the chalice was born.

As his bloodlust grew into frenzy, Vlad drank the blood of those he had impaled from a golden chalice. Daily, he supped the terrible potion from the chalice until he could no longer stomach food. Then, one day, in an act of perverse entertainment, he placed the chalice on the fountain in Tirgoviste, his capital, instructing all to drink freely from the golden cup, announcing that even the poorest of beggars could drink like a prince. But removal of the chalice would be answered by impalement. Such was his control, no-one dared to remove it; however poor, however great its value. It was on the day of its disappearance that the people of Wallachia knew that Vlad was dead.

At the end of the fourth crusade, Constantinople – the capital of the Byzantine Empire – fell leaving it vulnerable to looting and pillage by mutinous crusaders. They terrorized, and vandalized the ancient city for three days, some stealing ancient and priceless works of art. Betrayed by the Church and threatened with excommunication, some of the Crusaders violated the city's holy places and stole everything they could lay hands on, including sacred objects. The Crusader army sacked churches, monasteries and convents in their lust for glory and, it was from one of those important and sacred edifices that the chalice had been removed.

Eventually, it found its way into Vlad's possession – this golden chalice, studded with pigeon-blood rubies around its rim and foot – taken by blood and given to blood, it would be the instrument of Vlad's return.

Vasile contemplated the history of his ancestor; in particular, his death.

The biting, cruel, cold of Transylvanian winter had set in by December 1476 and Vlad had died in the forest at the hands of disloyal boyars of Wallachia, who were also fighting the Turks. It was widely believed that they cut off his head and sent it to the Sultan as proof of his demise and their loyalty. His decapitated body was then buried in the island monastery of Snagov, near Bucharest.

But Vasile Tepes knew the truth: Vlad Dracula's body lay in a vault beneath his fortress-home overlooking the ruins at Poenari, complete with its head still attached to its body.

In the dense forest just outside Bucharest, those loyal to Vlad had ambushed a peasant with the look of their leader – there were many that bore the Tepes features and illegitimate bloodline – and beheaded him, violating his face just enough to convince their enemies that it was indeed the body of the Impaler. The headless body was then dressed in Vlad's clothes and his ring bearing the seal of the House of Tepes placed on the dead man's hand.

It was the head of the peasant that was paraded and impaled by Vlad's enemies, and it was the peasant's body that was buried in the tomb of a prince.

Centuries had passed with Vasile at the head of the House of Tepes, in no hurry to resurrect his great-grandfather; enjoying, as he did, his power and wealth and unwilling to bow to another: even if he had the chalice – which he didn't. Documents in the hands of Vlad's son, Minhea, which told of the power of the chalice – so steeped in blood, that its very essence was of the life-force – were carefully hidden away after they were engraved on Vasile's consciousness. He knew there was a seal bearing the location of the chalice and, he also knew that it, too, was lost.

CHAPTER SIX: DRACULA'S CASTLE

Dan soon lost himself in the journal of Jonathan Harker as told by Bram Stoker and could easily see why the tale had inspired readers, film-makers and movie-goers for so long and – more importantly in his opinion – Lucy's unhealthy obsession. The description of Dracula's castle made him shiver and he began to look forward to Poenari, where he would be able to imagine the creepy castle rising from the ruins at the top of the rugged mountain. Lucy had fallen silent and sat back in her seat, absently fingering her necklace.

Christian stood up at the front of their coach and grabbed their attention through a small microphone.

"We'll soon be arriving at TIrgoviste, the former capital of Dracula's Wallachia, where you'll be able to see and climb the famous Chindia Tower, or, as it is translated in old Romanian, the Sunset Tower. Vlad the Impaler, Vlad Dracula, built the tower around which the impaled bodies of his enemies were displayed. I can't promise there will be any impaled transgressors today but you *will* get great views over the entire city and, before we leave, you will have time to wander around the ruins of his princely court. If you suffer from vertigo or any other form of dizziness I would recommend you don't climb the tower. The narrow steps spiral to the top at a very sharp angle, although there are three landings where you can take a breather. Afterwards we will have lunch in a local restaurant before moving on to Poenari and the ruins of the real Castle Dracula. If you think the tower was a tough climb, watch this space … there are fourteen hundred steps up to the ruins. If you don't want to make the climb there is a stall at the foot of the climb where you can buy a bottle of local red wine and sit back and relax. So, I'll shut up now for you to enjoy the scenery as we drive into Tirgoviste."

Dan raised his head from the book. "*Not* climb up to Dracula's lair? I don't think so," he laughed. "You know, Luce, reading this 'journal' gave me an idea. You should write a diary of the trip. Or you could drag yourself into this century and write it as a blog; you can use my tablet if you like. I mean, it's unlikely that we will ever come back again. Luce? Are you OK?"

Lucy looked pale. She smiled, trying to inject more sunshine into it than she felt – and it bothered her. This was a trip of a life-time and one she had awaited with joyous anticipation since they booked it ten months previously. Perhaps that was the problem … slight anti-climax after such frenetic expectancy. She smiled again, this time with more feeling. "I'm fine. Maybe a little tired, that's all. And, hell yeah, I'll race you to the top."

She let her necklace fall back against her chest, realising she was fingering it; something she did when worried or anxious.

Dan laughed. "Yeah, right. In your dreams. I'll be there waiting for you!"

Further conversation was interrupted by the beautiful scenery approaching the city and they were soon stepping from the coach in the shadow of the tower.

Neatly-clipped hedges flanked the path that led past the ruins of Vlad's court, stark in their dereliction, but covering a huge expanse and rearing up at the end of the path was the Chindia Tower.

The round tower appeared to be emerging from a truncated pyramid at its base, rising clean and clear to a height of twenty-seven metres – eighty-nine feet in old money – sixteen feet higher than its original reach, having been restored and added to in the nineteenth century.

Christian hadn't been kidding; the narrow, spiral stone steps wound their way sharply up the tower, passing small windows on their ascent. Half-way up, Lucy was suddenly overcome with a feeling of nausea. She put out a hand to steady herself. Dan was right behind her and put a supporting arm at her slim waist.

"Steady!" he said gently. "Take a break at the next landing. You don't have to go all the way up. I'll stay with you."

Lucy grinned at him, the nausea gone as quickly as it had struck. "I'm OK, it's just hot in here; all the bodies … people … in such a confined space. I expect. It's gone now. Come on, let's go look at the city."

The view from the top of the tower was, as promised, breath-taking and would have presented a perfect vantage point for Vlad Dracula to see the approach of his enemies. In contrast to the heat inside the tower, on the top and looking out over the surrounding country, the air was chilled. Autumn had a firm and welcoming grasp on the approaching winter and the crisp air made Lucy pull her calf-length cloak close around her. Dan had smiled at her new outfits that she had painstakingly stitched over the summer, especially the long, black, woollen cloak with its fake-fur lining. Well, he looked cold in his jeans and jacket, so she guessed he wasn't laughing now.

He was turning this way and that, walking around the top of the tower, taking pictures in every direction, and then he turned the camera on her. "Smile, please," he said in a sing-song voice.

She grinned. "Idiot!" She hated having her photograph taken and Dan knew it, but he was determined to capture everything for her. As they descended the steps, Lucy felt a prickle on the back of her neck; the feeling she always had when another person was staring at her. She turned quickly but the Goth girl behind her, Sally, had her eyes glued to the steep steps, watching every inch of where she was putting her feet. Lucy shrugged and did the same; a fall right at the beginning of the trip would be disastrous.

Back at the coach, Christian claimed their attention again. A beautiful Romanian woman stood next to him; tall and super-model thin. She wore knee-length boots over tight black pants and an over-sized, chunky, grey sweater with a roll-neck that sat just under her chin. Her shoulder-length, ebony hair framed her exquisitely made-up face and matched her flashing dark eyes. Lucy sneaked a look at Dan; he was obviously impressed with the newcomer so she dug him in the ribs, hard.

Christian was introducing the beauty to them.

"As you know, this is the last trip for this season but what you may not know is that the trips run weekly; one starting as another reaches the end. I'd like you to meet Davina who acts as guide on the alternate trip and has finished for the season so she will be joining us. *And ...*" he paused dramatically, then broke into a huge grin, "... she has just kindly agreed to be my wife!"

There was a spontaneous chorus of congratulation, mixed with whistles and catcalls from some of the men while Christian and Davina, wreathed in smiles, enjoyed their moment. Phones and cameras captured the image, including several selfies with the happy couple before boarding the coach for the ruined castle at Poenari.

The Transfagarasan Highway cut through the mountains to the Alpine area of the Carpathians, hugging the side of the mountains as it went. This was one of the roads that would be closed a week from then as winter set in.

The coach parked at the foot of the mountain and every face was lifted upwards to the ruins of Vlad's lofty sanctuary from the Turks. Everyone was up for the climb but Davina offered to stay behind in case anyone dropped out half-way.

Dan smiled at Lucy, "Race you to the top," and set off at a swift pace. The group quickly split up into those who were fit, and the stragglers. Lucy was somewhere in the middle, though she kept her eye on Dan, who turned around at intervals to wave to her. She was just becoming used to the climb when she suddenly tripped, apparently over nothing, and twisted her ankle.

Her cry of anguish was enough to bring the whole party to a halt, causing her major embarrassment. Dan was back with her instantly.

"Come on, I'll help you back to the coach." His arm was around her, supporting her, but she was mortified.

"No! No way. I can get back on my own, it's hardly any distance. There's no way you're coming all the way here and not seeing this. Besides you can take photos for me to see later. Davina is back at the coach and there was talk of red wine for those of us that couldn't make it. I'll be fine; I've hardly climbed any distance at all."

Dan looked unconvinced, but her glare was enough to let him know she felt stupid enough for having tripped in the first place, without making more of it than necessary.

"Hi, I saw you fall, are you OK?" Davina appeared behind them. "Come on, I'll help you down and Dan can carry on with the others."

Lucy beamed at her. "I'm fine, really, but I won't push it and try and climb on, I don't want to be limping for the rest of the trip. Thanks."

Davina gave her an answering grin and the two went back to the coach where there was indeed a bottle of local red wine. Conversation was easy and Lucy felt relaxed in her company as they chatted about the rest of the trip and Davina and Christian's forthcoming wedding. The pain in her ankle was already wearing off, along with her discomfort at suddenly being the centre of attention, however briefly.

There was a momentary lull in their conversation which Davina felt compelled to fill as Lucy sat fingering her necklace.

"That's an unusual necklace. Very pretty."

Lucy stopped fingering it. "It belonged to my grandmother; she always said it brought her luck. She had a lot of unusual things; Grandfather was a collector."

"Lucy, are you OK? Did you hurt yourself more than

you're saying?"

Lucy looked around her, a crease on her brow. "No …
no, I'm fine. It's the silliest thing; I just keep thinking that
someone is watching me."

CHAPTER SEVEN: SLEEPING BEAUTY AWAKES

Beckett's journey was made easy by the vampire network of services. He flew to Kozani airport in Greece and was met with a Jeep at his disposal. The drive to the small convent took less than an hour, but to him it felt as though he was never going to get there.

Eventually, the rolling hills that were draped in olive groves gave way to small hamlets and back into olive groves again. He was near his destination now; he could feel a constriction in his chest and a lump in his throat the size of a small grapefruit. *Would she wake up? Would it be the same? Would she be different?* He tried to put all these thoughts away and connect with her telepathically as all vampires could. Try as he might, he couldn't sense her consciousness, but his gut was telling him something was happening. He pressed harder on the accelerator.

The old, white-walled monastery sat on the dusty hillside, vacated years ago in favour of a more modern building that had been gifted to the monks. Sister Anna had lived in isolation in the old building, taking care of Lane as she slept in deep hibernation whilst healing from her horrendous wounds. Wounds inflicted in the battle against the vampires who wanted to eradicate all the Created, five years previously. Since then Lane had lain in the Long Sleep with Anna transfusing her own blood from time to time to keep her alive.

Beckett had made sure that she had everything she needed and had organised regular deliveries of food and wine, keeping in touch with her by phone on Lane's condition and making sure that Anna was in need of nothing. *She* had only called *him* once, and that was the previous day.

As the old white walls came into view, partially hidden from sight by a long-abandoned olive grove, Beckett's anxiety hiked up a notch.

Anna was waiting for him at the door.

"Hello Beckett, it's good to see you. Lane still sleeps but she appears much disturbed, tossing and turning and mumbling in her sleep, as if she is in a constant bad dream. I thought it best to call you."

Beckett ignored the nun's habit and wimple and hugged her, lifting her off the ground, and then he planted a kiss on her cheek, bringing a blush from her neck to her scalp.

"Anna, you are a very special person. I can't begin to thank you."

Anna dropped her head, unused to praise or appreciation. She had cared for Lane as though she were her own child and, since her old convent was destroyed and the couple of remaining nuns scattered to other Orders, it was all she had and she had loved every minute of her five-year long vigil.

"Come," she said, with a brilliant smile, "Let me take you to her."

Beckett swallowed hard and nodded as he followed her inside.

Lane lay where he had left her all those years ago. Only then she had been covered with blood and he had believed her to be dying. Lane, his mentor and love, though never his lover, now looked as though she was simply asleep. Her long auburn hair splayed out over the snow-white pillow and there was an aura of peace around her which Beckett knew was attributable to Anna's care.

Minutes later, however, she began mumbling and a frown settled over her forehead. Beckett couldn't make out her words but the images that shot into his head made him take a step back. She was trying to communicate something to him – what was it? Were they visions that she was sharing, or simply bad dreams? One face stood out in his inner sight; Vasile Tepes. He ground his teeth and closed his eyes, the better to try and see where he was. Suddenly, images of Vasile's mountain lair crept across his mental screen. Lane was 'seeing' this in her vampire sleep.

Anna put a hand on his arm. "Look, she moves."

Lane's hand was moving as she stretched out her fingers, then her arm moved. Beckett held his breath.

One thing he had learned was that you never try to wake a sleeping vampire; especially when they were in deep sleep to heal. She could be shocked into so deep a sleep that she would never wake. He sighed and took a step nearer to her, careful not to touch her – even though he yearned to pick her up and take her home; he had no idea how much she had healed already or if moving her would prove fatal still.

"Has she said anything?" he asked Anna.

Anna shook her head. "I can't make out what she is trying to say most of the time but I heard two things last night. She said 'Mihai' and she also said 'the Source'. This morning she appeared angry and I thought she said 'not a virus', though I could have been mistaken."

Beckett nodded his understanding, though he kept hidden his disappointment in the fact that it had been Mihai's name that she had said, and not his own.

Anna laid a gentle hand on his forearm. "I'll leave you with her. Just call if you need anything." And she left the room with a quiet rustle of her habit.

Beckett stood watching Lane in silence for several minutes and then took out his phone and hit a number on speed dial. It was answered very quickly.

"Beckett, I haven't heard from you for too long. Do you have news? Or is there a problem? How can I assist you, my friend?"

Despite his initial disappointment, Beckett smiled at Mihai's voice. He had been neglectful in not calling him but Mihai was now the Patriarch of the Vampire Council and obviously busy. Still, he had no excuse, except, as he now recognised, there was a tiny maggot of jealousy over Lane's obvious, long-standing friendship and love for Mihai. He hoped it was a different kind of love, even though Mihai had found love of his own in the geneticist, Dr Helena Bancroft.

"Hello, Mihai. I am truly sorry that I have not called you. I hope you forgive me." He was prevented further explanation as Mihai interrupted him.

"I sense you too are in Greece; she wakes?"

Beckett smiled. The ancient vampire's telepathic abilities were highly developed and it made things a whole lot easier – if occasionally disconcerting.

"Something is disturbing her, Mihai, she seems troubled. I think she will wake soon and I will be here when she does. I thought you should know; especially as she said your name last night." He waited for a response that took a few moments.

"Has she said anything else?"

Beckett frowned; he hadn't liked what her other words implied. "She also said 'the Source' and 'not a virus'. I don't like where this might be going. Not after all this time. It changes everything."

"Will you be offended if I come? I do know how you feel about her, Beckett. I assure you, I won't get in the way of that."

Beckett smiled; despite his early tiny pang of jealousy, he would be glad to see Mihai and whatever was troubling Lane was something big. He would be glad of company.

"It will be good to see you. Come whenever you want. I should tell you that I picked up on her thoughts and visions. Whatever is disturbing her, it involves Vasile Tepes."

He heard a sharp intake of breath before Mihai replied. "I'll come straight away; when Lane wakes she will be weak and vulnerable. It is good that you are there. I am also in Greece on Council business. You should know that Helena's work is not progressing as we had hoped."

Beckett disconnected the call and turned back to Lane, as he contemplated Helena Bancroft's work in trying to find a 'cure' for the vampirism in the Created. An hour passed without further movement or mumbling and she appeared serene again. He thought about her life; her very long life. Taken to live in the home of her uncle, Cosimo de Medici, in fifteenth century Florence and, practically forced into an abusive marriage, Lane had fallen foul of a predatory vampire. For over six hundred years she had walked the earth trying make it a better place for those similarly afflicted, and fighting those vampires that revelled in their power to prey on the innocent; those like Vasile Tepes.

Dark thoughts about what he would do to Vasile when their paths crossed again were interrupted as Lane let out a long, drawn-out sigh, and then she lifted a hand to her brow as if she had a headache. He moved closer to the bed, hardly daring to think that the moment he had waited for, for five years, was finally here. He swallowed the grapefruit-sized lump in his throat again and wiped a lone tear from the corner of his eye.

She opened her eyes and smiled. "Hello, Handsome," she whispered, using her affectionate name for him.

The heart of a vampire beats exceedingly slow, and Beckett was no exception, yet he could feel the organ lurch beneath his ribs.

"Hello, Legs. It's good to see you." His voice was casual but his emotions were in freefall.

CHAPTER EIGHT: IMPORTANT INFORMATION

Lucy Eastman's Journal

10th October 2016

I have had to pinch myself several times to realise that I am in Transylvania, the trip of my dreams, following in the footsteps of the historical Vlad Dracula – or 'Vlad the Impaler' and the fictional Dracula. At Dan's suggestion, I have begun a journal of our Transylvanian experience.

We arrived in Bucharest and were met by Christian, our guide for the trip, who took us to see the Chindia Tower, adjacent to the Princely Court of Vlad Dracula and around which Vlad impaled many of his enemies as he stood at the top to appreciate his work. I had to stop half-way up, overcome with nausea, which is odd because I have never suffered vertigo or a problem with heights before, though I eventually made it to the top.

Then, on to Poenari, Vlad Dracula's fortress home, now in ruins. Again, I was prevented from climbing up to the fortress after a stupid fall. Christian's fiancée, Davina, came to my rescue and we enjoyed a chat and some local wine whilst waiting for the others to return to the coach. It is probably nothing, but I had the disturbing sense of someone watching me.

Dan, who agreed to the trip mainly to please me, was unexpectedly excited on his return from the mountain fortress and immediately shared the many photographs he had taken of the breath-taking countryside.

My worry is that after so many years of longing to visit this country, reputedly the home of the vampire, that it will be an anti-climax. The rest of the group seem very nice and, like me, believe in the creature of the night and are very forthcoming about their love of the genre, in both literature and film, of which they are knowledgeable and enthusiastic. Dan has always simply tolerated what he calls my obsession, so it is good to have others that share my passion to talk to.

We left Poenari for our first overnight stop at the town of Sibiu, a beautiful medieval city of cobbled streets and squares and full of Vlad's history, having lived there from 1451 to 1456 after abandoning his birthplace of Sighisoara. I was feeling very tired suddenly and was impatient to check into our hotel. I hope I'm not coming down with something.

The Hotel Apollo Hermanstadt is lovely, and a short walk from the centre of Sibiu, so we were soon being shown into our rooms before dinner. I can't shake the tiredness, but look forward to the traditional meal of Paprika Hendl as enjoyed by the intrepid Jonathan Harker of *Dracula* fame.

Dinner was delicious. Essentially a chicken, tomato and paprika stew, it went some way to restoring my spirits. The others were for staying up late but I declined the invitation, needing sleep. I insisted that Dan at least stay and have a drink with them, not wanting to isolate us right at the beginning of the trip.

11th October 2016

I slept heavily and woke feeling un-refreshed but ready for the day, fuelled mainly by determination to love every moment of the trip. Breakfast was coffee and rolls, after which we pushed our luggage back into the hold of the coach – something we would do almost every day, living as we were out of our suitcases. This morning is freezing cold and I am glad of my warm fur-lined cloak. Today we are heading for Sighisoara, the birthplace of Vlad the Impaler. I wish I had a little more energy; I am so tired. The cold has been dispelled somewhat as the others passed around a flask of the local plum brandy.

*

Vasile Tepes was deep in thought when his old retainer entered his inner sanctum that sat vigil over the ruined fortress.

"Sir, there is a telephone call for you. They didn't give a name."

"Did they say what they want, Nicolae?"

"Something about a chalice in which you may have an interest."

Vasile said nothing, simply holding out his hand to receive the telephone as Nicolae made a discreet withdrawal.

"This is Vasile Tepes, to whom am I speaking?"

The voice on the other end of the conversation grabbed his attention and he listened without speaking for several minutes.

Eventually he said, "If this is true you will be rewarded. If it is not … well, let's hope this information is correct."

He disconnected the call and returned to his seat looking out through the huge picture window which framed the ruins across the Arges valley. After ten minutes of contemplation he rose suddenly and strode out of the room and down several staircases to the basement of his mountain retreat.

Vlad's shrine was placed centrally in the basement with huge candlesticks at each corner. His coffin sat on a marble plinth bearing carvings of the insignia of the Order of the Dragon and his family crest; images that were reflected in the ancient tapestries hanging from the stone walls.

Vasile lit the candles and stood to one side.

"Great-Grandfather, I have received information which may lead me to your chalice. Once I have it, you will be restored and take your place as the oldest of our kind and lead us against the abomination of the Created. Much has happened since you left so many centuries ago but I will be at your side to assist you in any way that I can. The House of Tepes and the name of Dracula will once again be feared throughout this country and beyond."

He turned quickly and left the candles burning, sending dancing lights and grotesque shadows onto the stone walls. Inside the coffin lay the body of the one they had called Vlad Dracula. Desiccated skin stretched, parchment-like, across the skull and wisps of dark hair were still visible. The eyes were closed but appeared sunken and the mouth gaped open, revealing two elongated and pointed canine teeth that gave the impression of a predatory grin.

The candles flickered and flared suddenly before being extinguished by an unseen hand.

Upstairs, Vasile pulled on an expensive overcoat and called for his car. He must see for himself if the information was correct and, if so, he would have to act swiftly.

CHAPTER NINE: VISIONS OR DREAMS

Lane tried to sit up but didn't have the strength to do so. Beckett put his arm around her back and lifted her as though she were a small child.

"You need to feed," he said.

Lane was weak after her vampire sleep and, although Anna had kept her supplied with her blood, it had only sustained her in sleep and in healing; now she needed more, much more.

"Call Anna," she whispered.

Beckett shook his head. "No," he said. "Not this time."

He pulled back his shirt sleeve of his free arm and bit into his wrist, his pointed canines puncturing the blood vessel with precision. The blood welled up and she smiled weakly as he allowed the crimson life-force to fall onto her lips and fill her mouth. She strengthened with each swallow and, in her hunger, she grabbed his wrist, sucking long and hard, stopping only when Beckett pulled his arm away.

"That's enough for now, honey – unless you want me to be in need of Anna's ministrations."

He grinned at her as she wiped away the blood from her chin, licking its residue from her fingertips, and then he looked away, unsure of her reaction to his emotions. They had only just begun to admit their feelings for each other moments before she had been brutally wounded five years ago and she had been asleep ever since then. She was obviously troubled but, as yet, he had no idea of the cause. Was it because she now felt differently? He cleared his throat.

"Lane, I … are you OK?"

She frowned. "I will be. But something is very wrong;

45

the visions were so intense. Beckett, the Born are planning another war – I know it – and if they aren't stopped, this world will become nothing more than their feeding ground and humans their food. It can't *be*. We can't let it!"

She was even paler than usual and Beckett could hear her heart pounding behind her ribs; his concern over their relationship gave way to fear. Lane never over-reacted but she was clearly very frightened.

He pulled her to him and hugged her as he planted a kiss on top of her head. The storm in his grey eyes upgraded to a hurricane. "We won't let it be," he said, into her hair; hair that, as he spoke, was regaining its familiar lustre. His blood was doing its job.

She leaned against him, resting her head on his chest for a moment longer than he anticipated; he closed his eyes and dared to hope. But there were other things more urgent now and he allowed them to take precedence.

When a vampire went into deep and healing sleep, they sometimes unwittingly connected to other vampire minds, especially the old ones. Beckett knew that any visions or prophetic dreams that Lane had experienced were to be taken very seriously. And Lane had begun to recall them all, slowly reliving everything she had seen.

"Vasile Tepes is behind all this. I saw him clearly. He is searching for something; something that will give him the power to lead the Born. I think it's a chalice … I can't … no, wait … Christ, he's looking for the golden chalice of Vlad Dracula! He can't be allowed to get his hands on it because, if he does, it will make him almost invincible … unless …" She tilted her face up to his and her expression was enough to tell Beckett that the 'unless' was not going to be good news.

"Unless?"

"Unless he plans to use it to try and bring back its previous owner." Her voice was tight and dry and her eyes reflected the panic she was feeling. "We need to speak to Mihai," she said.

"Mihai was already near here on Council business; he is on his way," Beckett answered. "He felt your awakening when I called him. I think he may also have some idea of what is going on; he seemed very uptight and more than a little cagey. Legs, are you trying to tell me that Vasile Tepes can use this chalice to resurrect Vlad? I thought all that was pure myth. Can he really be brought back from the dead? That's pure Hollywood and pulp fiction, no? Besides, they took his head and buried his body at Snagov."

She shook her head, "It's true, decapitation is it – the end – but there are some of us that think that wasn't the case and that it was never Vlad who was interred at Snagov. As for the chalice, Mihai's predecessor found evidence that it was hidden when it was removed from the fountain in Tirgoviste. We need to pray that it stays that way."

"Do you know where it is? Does anyone?"

She shook her head vigorously. "No. The one who took it did so because of its nature; the blood of thousands was drunk from it, until it was almost of the blood itself. After he hid it, they say he took his own life without telling another soul of its whereabouts."

"So, just say Vasile finds it, what good is it without Vlad's body, and what is so important about Vlad anyway? I would have thought that Vasile would want nothing more than to remain as head of the House of Tepes."

"Because, if he succeeds, Vlad will once again be the most powerful living vampire, and as such will command the respect and obedience of most of the Born. With him as their leader, there will be no mercy … and no survivors."

A deep, Eastern European accent claimed their attention. "Then, we must find it first." Mihai Rabinescu stepped into the room, leaving Anna, flapping and flustered, in his wake. "Lane, my dear, it's good to have you back amongst us. Are you healed?"

Lane nodded at him, allowing the swift embrace from the Patriarch of the Council and her oldest friend. "Yes, Mihai, I am whole again."

Apparently satisfied that his favourite was, in fact, healed, he turned to Beckett. "I believe we are all about to become very busy. You should attend to any worldly affairs and be ready."

Beckett nodded, his countenance solemn. "I'm ready, Mihai. But if the chalice is so well hidden, then why the urgency?"

"Because, while no other soul was *told* of the chalice's whereabouts, there is a seal that does just that. And it's missing."

Beckett's frown deepened. "So why make the seal at all? If the whereabouts of the chalice is such a secret, why make something which gives its location?" He turned to Lane. "Did you know of this chalice?"

She nodded. "Only by legend but, so much of Vlad's legend is mired in fiction along with elements of truth. As it is in all legends, you know that. "

"And the legend of the chalice?"

Mihai answered him. "It is the chalice that Vlad drank the blood of his victims from. The hidden lore about it is that one of his victims was one of the ancient vampires and by drinking his blood from the chalice, along with the curse that the vampire laid on him, is how Vlad became vampire in the first place. So potent was the vampire blood, it corrupted the chalice itself by leaving an indelible stain on the inside that contained the actual essence of the vampire."

Beckett was still processing. "So, if by drinking from the chalice, Vlad can somehow be restored – and I haven't even begun to go *there* yet – why didn't it affect the townsfolk of Tirgoviste that drank from it?"

Mihai's expression didn't change as he said in a lowered voice, "But it did; the latents that drank from it turned."

There was silence as Beckett and Lane digested the

information, then they both asked the same question simultaneously.

"How do you know the seal is missing?"

Mihai hesitated. "… Because it isn't where I left it."

CHAPTER TEN: HERO OR VILLAIN?

From Lucy Eastman's Journal

11th October 2016

Leaving Sibiu with a strange feeling that has nothing to do with the desolate image of the ruins of Vlad's castle from earlier in the day. I can't get rid of the feeling that I am being watched. I look at my fellow travellers and wonder which one.

I can't seem to concentrate on the stark beauty of the Carpathians, wanting only to sleep. Dan thinks that I am simply overtired and laughed at my feeling that someone was watching my every move. Perhaps it is nothing more than the atmospheric nature of the trip.

Sighisoara was the birthplace of Vlad Tepes and our next destination. It is a medieval citadel that would make a perfect picture postcard, with its cobbled streets, medieval walls, huge watchtowers and wonderful architecture. But, we are here to see the house in the cobbled square that is allegedly the house of Vlad Dracul and the birthplace of his son, Vlad III: Vlad Dracula. Increasingly I am thinking of Vlad and the fictional Dracula as one and the same.

It is clear that Vlad was, and still is, a hero to the Transylvanian people – his picture is everywhere – some are happy to identify him as the inspiration for Bram Stoker and they are more than happy to market him as Dracula, as tourism plays a huge role in their economy.

Dan seems a little distant. I feel guilty because I was the one who wanted this trip more than anything – he agreed to it just to make me happy – yet, it is Dan that seems enthused by everything and everyone on this trip. He is drinking more than he usually does and is very much a part of the group. I was a little jealous to begin with but now I don't have the energy for that.

This is the second night that I have gone to bed early, leaving Dan to join in the high-spirited 'vampire-themed' evening.

My long, black, silk 'coffin' skirt, with its bustle and net lining, hung on the back of the door, almost accusingly. I thought of the hours of stitching and planning and made a decision. I wanted to do nothing but sleep but I showered and applied fresh make-up, squeezed into the tight-fitting skirt and black corset-top, pulled on the elbow-length black satin gloves and went to join the others.

I had no trouble in locating them in the hotel, I simply followed the noise. Dark, heavy, Goth music was blaring from a room on the ground floor and I caught sight of Davina just inside the door.

As I approached, a feeling of dread overwhelmed me, I felt cold despite the obvious central heating in the hotel. I shivered, I remember that – shivering. I heard Dan laughing and prepared to be amused too, but as I passed through the doorway, I froze. Dan stood with his back to the wall with his arm around one of the single women – Sally, I think – and he was kissing her on the neck. Both were blatantly drunk.

I thought I had been discreet in my devastated withdrawal but I had only gone a few steps when Davina came after me. Had she been watching for me? Watching me?

She said that Dan was drunk and I should pay no attention and she hinted that I should perhaps be more sociable and a part of the group. She persuaded me to go back in with her, pushing a glass of the local plum brandy into my hand – the cause of Dan's condition, I thought.

Dan appeared flustered and was quickly at my side and, I was greeted with enthusiasm by the others. A few sips of the fiery, local spirit warmed me but couldn't dispel the feeling of quiet dread. This was stupid; I had to get a grip of myself and enjoy what I had looked forward to, seemingly forever.

Later, when I asked Dan about Sally, he told me I was paranoid. Perhaps he's right

Tomorrow we head for Bistrita for lunch at The Golden Crown; Paprika Hendl no doubt, another nod to Jonathan Harker, or to give it its anglicised name – Paprika Chicken. After a tour of the city we head over the Borgo Pass to Castle Dracula Hotel and the masquerade ball. The thought cheers me.

CHAPTER ELEVEN: DONORS

Lane was first to react to Mihai's statement.

"What do you mean, '*it wasn't where you left it?*' What are you saying, Mihai, old friend?"

"I'm saying: *I* made the seal. And I did so at the instruction of the one who made me, long before Vlad was an ink blot on his family tree."

It was then that Lane realised something, she had no idea of Mihai's true age.

He read her and laughed, "I was born to our world before the one you call 'Christ', walked the earth. I'm old!"

They all laughed and their spirits lifted.

Beckett was the first to break the silence. "So, this chalice, do you know its whereabouts?"

"Yes and no. My maker took it into a lengthy, vampire sleep. But, if the rumours are correct, he died at his own hand at the turn of this millennium."

Beckett persisted, "So, if *you* don't know, then perhaps no-one else does."

Mihai was thoughtful. "Sorry, Beckett, that's a false assumption. I don't know because I haven't been looking for it. Whoever *is* looking for it could be very close. And, as I said, the seal is missing."

Lane was about to speak when she suddenly doubled over in pain.

Beckett was at her side so quickly that even Mihai didn't see him move.

"What is it?" His voice betrayed his inner panic.

She gasped as another wave of pain hit her before collapsing against him. Mihai was at her side then too, as Beckett lowered her gently to the ground.

"How many donors?" Mihai demanded.

"Just one, a young nun, you remember her? She's the one who just let you in."

"Yes, and, knowing Lane, she didn't take from her often enough. She needs to feed."

"I fed her when she woke," Beckett muttered, as he began to push up his sleeve.

Mihai stopped him, shaking his head slowly. "You can't do it again so soon. It has to be me."

Beckett's eyes were wide and his face displayed myriad emotions as he realised that Mihai was right. He nodded and bent to lift Lane, pulling her into a sitting position, leaning her against his chest. He could feel her heart slowing its already slow beat.

"Better hurry, then."

Mihai understood him instantly; with no time for refinements he tore open his sleeve and, canines down and ready for action, he tore into his wrist and held it over Lane's mouth.

The first drops landed on her motionless lips and ran down her chin. Beckett gently opened her mouth and watched as Mihai's ancient blood welled into it. She swallowed once, then again, and then opened her eyes.

She hesitated, so Mihai commanded her, "Drink!"

He lowered his wrist to her mouth and she drank – drank the most ancient of their blood; blood which was of the line of the First One. And with it went his ancient knowledge and his power. Beckett could almost feel it; Lane now had the most ancient of vampire blood in her veins and the power and knowledge of the ancients would grow in her with every deliberate beat of her heart.

She opened her eyes. Normally the darkest brown of ancient bog-oak, the irises of her eyes were now jet black and the whites were laced with red. Her body, still weak from hunger after her vampire sleep, had responded to the inflowing of the ancient blood in dramatic fashion. Was this to be the moment she was lost to him, Beckett wondered? Deep though their relationship had become, there had always been the fear of loss. Now that all the knowledge of the First One surged through her consciousness, would she still feel the first stirrings of love that had marked their last moments before she had drifted into five years of oblivion?

She sighed and Beckett felt her body relax into his. He cradled her head against him, hardly daring to hope.

Mihai took a step away and watched the wound on his wrist begin to heal. He had done the unthinkable. He had transferred some of the blood of the First One, a forbidden act and one that he would be answerable for – if any of the Ancients were still walking the earth.

His thoughts drifted to the First One, his maker and mentor.

Images of Ancient Egypt and the familiar scents of the temples filled him, comforted him. Intoxicating scents of rising incense smoke and the tinkling sound of tiny cymbals in the hands of the nubile women played in his ears and he closed his eyes, content for now to bathe in the memories that were usually held at bay.

Lane sat upright; the red lacing in her eyes had faded, revealing the jet black centres that would never leave her. The surge of telepathic senses, thoughts and visions from Mihai would also lose their intensity, though never fade completely. The ancient knowledge, however, would remain always.

She jumped to her feet with an energy that took hold of her suddenly, bringing Mihai back to the present with a jolt and sending Beckett's thoughts into the stratosphere as he leaped to his feet with her.

She turned on Mihai. "You knew! You knew that Vlad Dracula's body wasn't interred at Snagov – Vasile has him! If he gets hold of the chalice there is no hope for the Created – for any of us!"

Further words were halted as Beckett's phone rang in his pocket, bringing them all down a notch or two on the tension scale. He glanced at the number on the screen.

Why, in God's name, would Mike Travis be calling him when he knew he was in Greece?

"Mike? Not great timing. Can I get back …?" He stopped, went even paler than usual and slowly, very slowly, sank back onto his knees.

CHAPTER TWELVE: THE GRAND TOUR

Mike hadn't waited long for Darius to arrive and he greeted him with a warm smile. He had met him on several occasions and taken to him instantly, but those occasions had been when he had visited Beckett for his professional help, therefore their contact had been brief.

He knew nothing of Darius's background except that he wasn't vampire. He knew also that he was a loved and trusted assistant to Beckett, and that was a good enough character reference for anyone.

Darius greeted Mike as if he were an old friend. "Hi, sorry if you had to hang around. Did you hear? Lane is waking up!" The joy on his face completed Mike's impressions of the woman that, it was obvious, Beckett loved. He could see a different kind of love shining in the adoration in Darius's eyes. Mike smiled and nodded.

"So," Darius enthused, "have you seen everything? Beckett was giving you the grand tour, wasn't he? He told me to look after you and tell you everything you wanted to know about The Sanctuary. He was going to, anyway. Or would you prefer me to take you home?"

"I'm in no hurry," Mike said. He knew if there was any change in Beth's condition, either way, Roman would call him immediately and, besides, he liked Darius instinctively and wanted to know more about him. Apart from the sparkle of youthful adulation when he spoke of Lane, Darius obviously cared deeply for Beckett, like a son would.

"Unless I'm keeping you?" Mike continued.

Darius shook his head. "No. I was coming here anyway; keeping an eye on things. We can use Lane's sitting room and you must say when you are ready to go home." He led Mike back to Lane's room, pausing at the reception desk.

"It's quiet tonight, but I'm staying for a while. You know where I'll be if you need me."

The Goth girl nodded at him and returned to her book.

In the sitting room, Darius flicked a switch and the gas fire burst into blue and yellow flame. It wasn't cold, but he sensed Mike's need for comfort. He leaned over the elegant, low table and poured a healthy shot of whisky into a sparkling crystal glass and grinned at Mike.

"While the boss is away … enjoy!"

Mike allowed himself a small laugh; something that was rarer than angels in hell recently. The boy's youthful enthusiasm must be rubbing off on him. He sipped at the very old, single malt whisky from one of the oldest distilleries on the Scottish islands.

"Beckett pretty much gave me the low-down on this place. Impressive to say the least – and an eye-opener. I had begun to think I had seen most everything; I was wrong and I'm humbled. Actually, Darius, it's you that interests me. We've met occasionally but I'd like to know you a little better. If that's okay?"

Darius was thrown off-guard by this; more used to living in Beckett's shadow – in a good way – he had been prepared to talk Mike through the routine and not-so-routine operating of The Sanctuary, not to talk about himself. He appeared flustered.

Mike took another sip of the fiery, liquid gold that mellowed on contact with the back of his mouth and gave way to an earthy, smokiness.

"I'm sorry; that was rude of me. I've embarrassed you."

"No! No, not at all, I was surprised that's all. There really isn't much to tell in fact. I'm Beckett's assistant and, for '*assistant*' read '*does everything else*'." He laughed, but Mike saw through the bravado, that Darius did '*everything else*' for Beckett because he wanted to and not because he was employed to. He wanted even more to get to know him.

"Do I hear the remains of an Eastern European accent?"

"I was born in London, but my parents had only just arrived from Budapest. Our neighbours and friends were all Hungarian and, though we integrated with our British friends and neighbours, the accent somehow stuck. Both my parents and my … brother … are dead. Beckett is all I have really. Don't get me wrong; I'm not sad or looking for sympathy, life is what it is. I'm lucky to have Beckett and Lane. They are my family now."

Mike settled back against the gold silk brocade of the sofa and sipped his whisky, saying nothing, allowing Darius to untangle the threads of his history.

"My brother was a vampire of the most cruel and ruthless kind. He killed my parents and I spent years trying to track him down, with the intention of killing him. I believed myself to be a Hunter. I knew nothing. I found my brother's nightclub, Danse Macabre, here in Newport and lay in wait for him one night. I took the elevator to his apartment above the club and stood in the shadows for however long it would take. The elevator door opened and I wasted no time in thrusting an Ash stake into the heart. The only problem was, it wasn't my brother; it was Lane and I almost killed her. Luckily, Beckett and another vampire were outside and they saved her. I have never been so thankful for something in all my life. After Beckett threatened extreme bodily violence against me and advised putting a great distance between us, he began listening to my side of things. And even though I had almost killed her, Lane gave me a home and a job. It's been just Beckett and me for a while now, but it will be a relief to have Lane home again. And, you are right, he's very special to me; he calls me 'Son'. So, there you have it; Darius in a nutshell!"

Mike took another sip of whisky. "I think there's a lot more to you than that. But thanks for sharing. I see why Beckett cares for you."

Before Darius could reply his phone rang, the telephone on the low table rang and, outside in the hall, phones were ringing, alarms were shrieking and the front door entry system buzzed, flew open and a self-propelled missile in the form of a young woman wearing a military-style coat over tight black jeans and knee-high boots, crowned with a black top-hat over her impossibly black hair, shot inside at speed. Her face was smeared with blood and her clothes bore the same sanguineous stains. Her face was deathly pale that owed nothing to her Goth make-up.

Her voice was high-pitched and laden with panic. "Where is Beckett? Help me! Help all of us! They're coming!" The next second she had collapsed in a heap at Mike's feet.

CHAPTER THIRTEEN: ATTACK ON THE SANCTUARY

Darius was galvanised into action and ran towards the reception desk, where the emergency electronic locks were hidden from sight. He was only half way across the huge room when the door burst open again and three thugs, loyal to Vasile Tepes and his House, were inside before he or Mike could gather their thoughts.

Mike was bending over the inert young woman, relieved that she was breathing. It took him only a heartbeat to see that the blood splatters all over her had not come from any wound of hers and, satisfied she would recover, he sprang to Darius's side.

The young receptionist was pale and shaking, standing behind the desk in shock.

Three against two is crappy odds at the best of times but, when two of the three are vampires lusting for blood, well, someone is going to get hurt – bad.

Mike threw himself onto the nearest of them, who was lunging at him with a savage-looking blade. Blades, Mike could deal with – his attention was more on the snarling mouth with fangs ready for action.

He side-stepped the blade and brought his arm up, defending his throat as he swung his fist towards the offending maw. His knuckles split open as they made contact with the vicious fangs and he swore, loud and meaningfully, casting doubt on his attacker's lineage. A fleeting glance at Darius fending off the second blood-drinker and his attention was back full-on to his own plight. He swung his fist again but lost his balance and hit the floor with such force it knocked the breath from him. The last thing he saw before oblivion was the triumph on the face of his attacker as it loomed over him, his intention clear.

Images swam in his unconscious mind: Beth and their daughter Adain were playing happily on a beach. Suddenly, from nowhere, the image of a demon watching them, coming closer, loomed onto his mental screen. He cried out in silence as the image faded into an ocean of crimson. He felt as if he were floating on a red sea and, somewhere in the background, there was a curious sucking sensation at his throat.

His senses began to return slowly and he could smell smoke. What was this? Another unconscious game that his mind was playing? The smell of the smoke intensified and he felt the burning in his throat. And then the heat.

His eyes were open and his comprehension was instant. The Sanctuary was on fire. He leaped to his feet and peered through the smoke, covering his nose and mouth, coughing until his lungs felt as though they would burst into flame too.

Darius was lying on the floor, still and silent, with a gash at his throat that had strangely ceased to pump blood. Mike felt an icy claw around his heart as he dragged him towards the door. Feeling for a pulse on the uninjured side of Darius's neck, he felt it – weak and feeble but present. And then he saw it – the blood that was covering Darius's mouth and chin – the blood that he had been forced to drink from one of Vasile's vampire henchmen.

He cursed again, this time at his own lack of knowledge. He had no idea what to do for him.

He ran to the inert body of the dark-haired beauty who had raised the alarm; maybe she would know how to help Darius. She too was breathing and, as he touched her, she sat bolt upright, coughing, her eyes streaming. He left her and ran towards the reception desk, cloaked now in a pall of smoke. The young receptionist lay on the floor behind it, eyes open in death, her throat open, glistening in gore and her chest soaked in her own blood.

The entire room was alight now and raging flames filled the stairwell, preventing Mike from running towards the screams that were coming from one of the rooms on the first floor. He remembered the receptionist telling Beckett that there was a fledgling vampire there for help. There was no help for him now.

He turned back towards Darius as a beam crashed down on him, rendering him unconscious again and this time there were no dreams or visions, just oblivion.

The darkness shifted momentarily as searing heat hit his throat but, unconsciousness was so swift in its return he had no time to react to the pain. Blackness enveloped him again.

When the blackness faded and awareness gradually seeped through, the first thing that Mike saw was Roman Woolfe bending over him, concern etched into every pore of his face. He took a step back as Mike opened his eyes.

"Welcome back," he said, his voice grave. "You gave us quite a fright."

Mike gingerly raised his hand towards the massive lump on his head. A gentler hand prevented it from making contact. He turned towards the owner of the hand and flashes of lightning passed through his head, leaving a wake of nausea. He closed his eyes and then, as memory returned, he tried to sit up. Unhindered this time, he made it and leaned back against soft pillows.

"This admirable young lady has explained what happened. Incidentally, when you're better we need to have a discussion about going off on your own without leaving word of your whereabouts and perhaps you will take the time to report on this support network for vampires that we seem to know nothing about. At least you had your phone switched on, and she answered it when I called. You might like to thank her, Mike; she saved your life."

Mike grinned at her, about to voice his gratitude, and then as more memory asserted itself, his expression changed.

"Darius!" he exclaimed, "and those young people!"

He tried to get out of the bed. The restraining hand returned.

"He's here, Mike" she said. "I'm afraid there was nothing I could do for the others, but Darius is here, though I'm not too sure where 'here' is. But … he's in a bad way. I'm afraid he's turning."

Mike frowned. He didn't understand; his brain was still too fragile to interpret her words into anything that made any sense. His shook his head, and regretted it instantly.

"He was bitten … and force-fed vampire blood. From what I can tell, he is in the first stages of the turning. He's quiet at the moment but, soon … soon he will be in exquisite agony and I'm afraid I know nothing about how to help him. He needs Beckett. Where is he?"

Mike groaned. Beckett's love for the young man had been obvious, the love of a father for his son, for son Darius was in all but blood. Now another kind of blood was raging in his veins. Beckett had to be told. He swallowed the bile in his throat.

"How long have I been here?" he asked suddenly.

Roman answered him. "You've been out for eleven hours now, Mike."

"Then Beckett is in Greece," he said. His thoughts began to assemble themselves into comprehension and he raised his hand to his own throat, flinching at the sore, puckered flesh beneath his touch.

The girl nodded at him. "Yes, you were bitten, but you didn't drink from him. I cauterised the wounds with a burning piece of wood. You won't turn but I'm afraid you're going to have another scar," she said nodding towards the lengthy scar down his cheek. "Looks like you're used to being in the wars."

He shrugged. "I have to call Beckett. I feel responsible; I was there with Darius when this happened. The Sanctuary is burned out, I gather?"

She nodded. "Yes, it's nothing but a blackened shell now."

Further talk was halted as Darius's scream of torture ripped through the sombre atmosphere. Mike paled and reached for his phone, and his saviour rushed out of the room towards Darius's agony.

He tried to gather his words as he listened to the distant ringing of Beckett's phone, then Beckett's tense voice.

"Mike? Not great timing. Can I get back …?"

Mike interrupted him. "Beckett, listen to me. Something's happened here – something bad. I'm afraid Darius is hurt – well, more than hurt and, we don't know what to do to help him. Tell us what to do." He went on to describe the events at The Sanctuary, acutely aware of the silence at the other end – silence that was eventually broken by a woman's voice.

Unseen by Mike, Lane had caught the tumbling information running through Beckett's head.

"Oh God – Darius!" she exclaimed.

Another voice, a man's this time, came down the line. Mike could only assume that the news had sent Beckett into silent shock.

"This is Mihai Rabinescu, a friend of Beckett's. To whom am I speaking?"

"My name is Mike Travis, I'm calling from South Wales and I too am a friend of Beckett's. I'm afraid I just gave him some grave news."

"Yes, we understand. This news is devastating. How long ago did this happen?" he demanded.

Mike didn't give a thought to the fact that Beckett had voiced none of the news he had imparted or how Mihai Rabinescu, whoever he was, knew everything that had occurred. The whole vampire thing was beyond him. For now.

"About twelve hours ago," he replied, mentally calculating how long it would have taken for Roman

Woolfe to reach him and return to Linwood House.

Mihai's voice was stone. "Then I'm afraid there is nothing to be done for Darius other than being with him and minimising his pain. Every turning is different in how long it takes to manifest, but one thing is certain; he will very soon be in unimaginable agony. With the Sanctuary burned out, you will have to use your ingenuity to obtain some heavy-duty pain relief for him. A hospital is out of the question and it may take too long for me to make the necessary arrangements."

Mike glanced at Roman, "I think that will be easy enough," he said.

There was a pause on the other end of the conversation. "And then there will be another problem," Mihai said quietly.

"And that is?" Mike asked, already dreading the reply.

"And then Darius will be hungry. You take my meaning."

Mike took his meaning. "I'm rather afraid I do," he said before disconnecting the call.

CHAPTER FOURTEEN: THE MASQUERADE BALL

Vasile Tepes smiled with satisfaction as he heard news of the success of the mission to The Sanctuary. He was disappointed that the object of his fury had not been present, although he had known of her deep vampire sleep, he hadn't known Lane's location, cloaked as she was from him. He had hoped she would have been sleeping in some remote part of The Sanctuary but, never mind; there would be no sanctuary now for the filthy Created, or anyone else, there. News also began to filter through of other safe-houses and sanctuaries throughout Europe: Berlin, Paris, Madrid, Amsterdam, Budapest, Prague and Moscow, that had all suffered the same fate, being engulfed in flames with maximum casualties.

The war had begun.

He donned a thick overcoat and left his home, acknowledging his servant, Nicolae, in silence as he left. The heavy, oak door slammed behind him as he climbed into the driving seat of his sleek black limousine. He had no need of Nicolae; this was something for him alone. If the information he had received had been correct, this would certainly be a day for celebration.

He cast a glance across the valley to the ruins perched on top of the crags at Poenari. "Soon," he muttered to himself. "Soon."

He threw the car into gear and, well-used to the wintry mountain roads, he was on the main highway, heading towards the Borgo Pass, in minutes. The name of his destination irked him. *Castle Dracula Hotel*, a magnet for mindless tourists in his opinion, who dared associate themselves with his noble ancestor; thriving as they did on

69

cheap thrills from books and movie screens and playing at vampires. They would soon have more respect for the House of Tepes.

Delicate snowflakes had begun to drift over the Borgo Pass, despite the local peasantry being convinced that it would be another week or so before the sub-zero white blanket would isolate them from the rest of the world. In the distance a wolf howled, announcing its intention of leaving the forest in search of more readily available food.

Vasile smiled again. Today was a good day.

The long, winding drive to the hotel was already coated in a fine, white dusting of the early snow and, now the flakes were becoming thicker, coating the windscreen between the rhythmic sway of the wiper-blades. Yes, a good day indeed. Soon there would be no escape for the one he searched for. He would be generous to his informant.

Inside the hotel, against his better judgement, Christian had arranged for the Masquerade Ball to proceed in a minor form, despite the small group. Now, it was snowing contrary to the forecasts – both peasant and meteorological – and his instincts were to get the party back to Bucharest while he still could. He stood in the doorway looking up into the snow falling out of the early darkness. The drive was no longer visible; the dark tarmac now a white ribbon set in a white blanket.

The headlights of the approaching car created a diamond sparkle on the ground and the lying snow crunched under the tyres. He shielded his eyes against the glare of the headlights and wondered at the foolhardy action of the driver. He was already regretting his delay and decided to call off the party and instruct everyone to pack and be ready to leave within the hour.

The driver of the car seemed to be in front of him without leaving any footprints in the snow. He blinked and turned around to face Vasile who had somehow managed to appear behind him.

From the flanking forest came the howl of a wolf, answered almost immediately by another.

One of the ancients, Vasile was adept at infiltrating and controlling the minds of the unwary. He wasted no time in reaching into Christian's head.

There is one in your party that I seek. Take me to her. Now. Vasile transferred the image of the one he was looking for and followed Christian inside the hotel.

The vastly scaled-down Masquerade Ball was under way in one of the ground-floor rooms. Each had a mask of varying design; from spectacle-type eye- masks adorned in dramatic black feathers or similar plumage, to half or full-face masks that would be at home in any assembly in Venice. The six women all wore gothic gowns and the men were dressed in frock-coats and white shirts, with cravats and flowing lace cuffs appropriate to the gothic era. Byron himself would have been proud of their attire. All were happily imbibing the local plum brandy with differing degrees of enthusiasm; it was an acquired taste, the acquisition of which varied from person to person. From first glance, Vasile could tell that intoxication was imminent; it would make things easier.

One of the women detached herself from the group and approached him. Her ruby silk gown rustled pleasingly as she moved and Vasile took time to appreciate her slender figure encased under the corset-type bodice. Her eyes were behind a mask of peacock feathers but he reached into them with ease. She hesitated.

Christian stood beside Vasile, his eyes glazed and uncertain.

"Davina?" he muttered.

She ignored him and moved in close to Vasile, whispered something in his ear, and then kissed him long and slow on the lips before stepping back.

Vasile raised a hand and, without knowing why, everyone ceased their conversations and turned to face him. All were silent.

All were still.

All were afraid.

No-one moved.

Vasile pointed towards one of the women and beckoned. "You. Come here!"

The woman in the black satin ball gown with a mask of feathers the colour of a raven's wing stepped forward. Her fingers were at the pendant around her neck. She had always known that this time would come; her grandmother had told her so. She had kept it safe all those years, never taking it from around her neck; her touchstone, she called it, fingering it in moments of anxiety as if it would take away all burdens when *it* was the burden all along.

She glanced sideways at Dan, willing him to step in to protect her, but he looked away. She had known deep down that when the time came he would fail her, so she did the only thing she could do; she kept walking towards the commanding voice. As she stood in front of him, Vasile hooked a finger under the delicate chain and yanked the pendant from her neck. She was no longer afraid of him – rather she saw herself moving towards a destiny she had always dreamed of; to enter into the real world of the vampire. No more fantasy; no more role-playing. This was for real, and she held all the cards. Dan had let her down when she had wanted him to step up, now she had nothing to lose. Now, she would be one of them.

Vasile looked down at the necklace in his hand and his face suffused with rage.

"What is *this*?" he bellowed.

Lucy stood firm, a half-smile playing around her mouth. "*This* is half of what you are looking for. You can have it, but it will do you no good without the other half. Take me with you and I'll tell you where to find it."

Dan gave a small gasp. "Lucy … no;" he whispered.

Vasile's eyes narrowed into cruel slits. "You think I can't make you tell me?"

"I'm sure you can, but I'm not afraid of you. I'm sorry

Dan," she said. "I'll be leaving now."

Time was halted as the other members of the group tried to decide if this was part of the entertainment or for real, and if it *was* real, just *how* real. Any suspension of belief regarding vampires was about to get a severe going-over.

Vasile's mouth twisted into a savage grin as he grasped the pendant in the palm of his hand. Only half of the seal it may be, but his vampire senses and his psychometric skills were absolute and, he knew without a doubt who had created the seal. Mihai Rabinescu. And he also knew without doubt that Lucy had no idea where the other half was. He had no need of her.

But he would enjoy her.

He pulled her close to him, inhaling her perfume, feeling the soft skin of her neck against his lips, feeling it give under the tiniest hint of pressure from the sharp canines that were seeking out her jugular vein, sensing her longing for the oblivion and rebirth that would come when he made her vampire. She had no idea that such an act was abhorrent to him; that it would be the one thing he would deny her.

He pulled away and she gasped her disappointment.

Reaction among the others varied with their expectations. Christian's mind was still locked in a fog of confusion, Davina made a small sound of jealous protest and the others, beginning to sense the reality of their situation, made a sudden rush towards the door.

Vasile and Davina were on them in a millisecond, blocking the doorway with discarded, ripped bodies. None had the time to comprehend their fate before their throats were torn open.

Christian found himself unable to move; his face was ashen and he was shaking violently. Davina wiped the blood and gore from her chin and licked her lips and, taking a step forward she hit him hard across the face, sending him reeling against the wall. She was on him in seconds, dragging him from the heap of bodies and hauling him before Vasile.

He lifted his head towards her, terrified and heart-broken. "Davina," he whispered. "My God."

She grabbed his hair roughly and yanked his head back further as Vasile approached.

"Look at me," the head of the House of Tepes intoned, his voice steady and haunting. "Look at me."

Christian had no choice but to comply, his mind already belonging to Vasile.

"Davina will help you to get this mess into the coach along with their belongings. You will then clean up this room and take the coach down the mountain where you will drive it over the ravine into the gorge below where you will all be hidden under the snow until the spring, after providing much needed food for the wolves if they find you first. Do you understand?"

Tears were forming in Christian's eyes but they didn't fall. He simply nodded in silence as his instructions took possession of him.

Vasile grabbed Lucy's arm and dragged her whimpering towards the door.

"Vasile!" Davina's voice made him halt. "You promised me," she cried. "You promised me that it would be me at your side if I gave you the information you needed."

Vasile snarled at her. "Do as I have instructed and I may grant you access to my House. But disobey me or fail me and ..." he glanced meaningfully at the pile of bleeding death at his feet. His eyes flashed with unfettered power and she backed away to do as she was bid.

CHAPTER FIFTEEN: TENSIONS RUNNING HIGH

Despite having drunk the Blood of the First One once-removed via Mihai, Lane was still physically weak from her long vampire sleep. She laid a hand on Mihai's arm, concern for the lover of her old friend surging through her.

"Where is Helena?"

Dr Helena Bancroft, the red-haired, elfin-featured haematologist and geneticist who was desperately seeking a 'cure' for the vampire virus, was the love of Mihai's immortal life and her lab was an annexe to The Sanctuary.

Mihai exhaled a lengthy breath. "She wasn't in her lab. She was in Scotland doing some research that she hoped might lead to a breakthrough. She's safe, Lane, don't worry. Though it seems there is nothing left of The Sanctuary or her lab. I'm so sorry."

Lane sighed, long and hard. Her consuming passion for the protection of the Created fledgling vampires had led her to The Sanctuary project; a safe-house where newly-turned vampires could find help and care during the turning and, afterwards, where they could find supplies of the necessary blood that they required to stay alive. Not many survived the turning unless they were lucky enough to be brought to The Sanctuary. Many other Council members had followed her lead and 'sanctuaries' had sprung up all over Europe and had begun to do so in the Americas. What Lane had begun had become part of the vast vampire network. Now her dream was in charred ruins.

She sighed again and then drew herself to her full height. What had been created once could be so again,

75

though her heart was heavy for the casualties: the receptionist, the volunteer, and the newly-turned male vampire seeking refuge and finding only death.

But most of all she burned with rage for Darius; her Darius; Beckett's Darius. There would be a reckoning.

Beckett had been galvanised into action and while, in her weakened state, Lane grieved, Beckett had made arrangements for the swiftest return to Wales. To Darius. He had called Mike back and given rudimentary instructions for Darius's care but, he was in no doubt that, without immediate administration of the anti-HVV serum, Darius would turn and, bereft of the facilities in The Sanctuary that was now inevitable.

At least he had Mike and the facilities at The Strazca headquarters and, he understood that one of the volunteers, a Goth girl called Raven, who had been recruited from medical school at the University Hospital in Cardiff, was with him too. He hoped it would be enough; the turning took many lives.

Mihai had been deep in dark thought and then he broke his unaccustomed silence. "It has begun then; there is war between The Born and The Created. Blood is going to flow like a river before this is ended. We must be prepared for what is now inevitable. And we must find the chalice before Vasile Tepes does. He must not lay hands on it – whatever it takes."

Beckett understood his meaning but shook his head, his voice steady, his expression dark. "No Mihai, you keep your hands off him – he's mine."

Mihai simply nodded his understanding.

Lane seemed unaware of the lone tear that had escaped her eye and was pooling on her chin. Memories that had drifted in her subconscious mind during her long sleep were beginning to surface. She tilted her head as if to better 'hear' the information tumbling around inside.

"Mihai, I remember something. If I'm right, then Helena is wasting her time and it's no wonder she is getting nowhere. All this time we have believed we were fighting some kind of virus. It's not. It's a genetic mutation in the Born and one that is switched on when a victim is fed by its creator. We must speak to her as soon as possible."

Mihai nodded, "Yes, but there are more urgent matters, Lane. The chalice."

Beckett's eyes darkened even further. "More urgent than a cure? More urgent than Darius?" he demanded. "You know Mihai, it seems to me that someone who created the original seal, however misguided, should know what it looked like; should be able to reproduce it. Or am I mistaken?" The edge in his voice was palpable.

"What are you saying?" Mihai snapped.

Beckett shrugged. "Just asking a question, that's all. Do you have a problem with that?"

Mihai was furious and lost no time in displaying the fact. "How dare you? I have told you; I created the seal centuries ago on the specific instructions of my maker. That does not mean I would do so now. I can scarcely remember the seal; do you think I have not tried to recall the details?" he demanded.

Beckett persisted as the tension between them grew. "Perhaps, Patriarch, you should try harder. You imply that you remember some of the seal."

"Hey! Enough, you two! The war is between the Born under Vasile Tepes and the Created, not between us. Beckett, apologise, and Mihai, calm down please."

Mihai didn't speak for several seconds as he tried to compose himself. Beckett turned away as he said, "I apologise, Patriarch."

"Accepted," Mihai muttered, though both of them knew that something had been lost; some sense of kinship tainted.

Lane turned to Mihai. "Mihai, my oldest friend, is there nothing you remember of the seal?"

He softened perceptibly, which annoyed the hell out of

Beckett. "Of course I do, though the clue to the chalice's whereabouts was copied from a drawing by my maker all those centuries ago. He told me to make no copy, and to remove it from my memory. I obeyed. That was then, this is now."

"What does the seal look like, at least?" Beckett asked.

Mihai made an impatient gesture. "It was a gold disc inscribed with a dragon, wings unfurled, holding the chalice. Truly, that is all I remember. The clue to its location is inscribed on the back."

Lane pressed him further. "You said that it wasn't where you left it, where was that? Maybe if we start there we can work it out."

"I left it in a holy place, a bloody place, a place of worship, torture, death and imprisonment. I left it with the monks on Snagov Island."

Beckett checked his watch, impatient to get back to Darius. "I estimate the car will be here in around 3 minutes, then I'm leaving. Darius needs me. He needs us." He looked significantly at Lane.

"The responsibility is mine," Mihai said, in an even tone. "I will find it and I will find the chalice. In the meantime, I will send Helena to Darius, she may be able to help – if it's not too late already."

Lane nodded at Beckett; he was right, their priority was Darius and The Sanctuary, but she was curious. "Why Snagov? Surely that was his burial place. Why would you leave it so close to him? And who would have taken it from there? "

Mihai had begun to pace. "Because it's exactly the last place anyone would expect me to have hidden it! Snagov's history is both spiritual and blood- stained, as I said. There were two chapels on the isolated island, one built by Vlad's grandfather and one by Vlad himself; his is the only one remaining. Vlad converted the poorly defended monastery into an island fortress, satisfying his morbid need for refuge. It was ideal, surrounded by dense forests and only accessible by boat with a clear view on all sides. Folklore says that his henchmen put his treasure into barrels and tossed them into the lake to keep it from the Turks, a service for which they were promptly impaled. It still hasn't been found to this day. He imprisoned his enemies and tortured, impaled and beheaded them in a tiny cell in the monastery. Soon after Vlad's death, a huge storm erupted and tore the other chapel from its foundations and blew it into the lake; Vlad's final revenge. In the middle of the nineteenth century, the then-governor of Wallachia converted it into a state prison which was abandoned after twenty years and finally closed in 1867. The whole place was pillaged; tombs violated, bricks, stones, roof timbers and windows – all looted. That was when the seal was taken. Supposed grave-finds were taken to the History Museum in Bucharest, and have since mysteriously disappeared. Sold onto the black market probably, which means the seal could be anywhere. Snagov was restored eventually."

They both heard the weariness in his voice and both pondered his true age. He had lived since the dawn of civilisation and slept for centuries at a time. He had the right to be weary.

Mihai continued his pacing, his words sounding increasingly distant as he gave voice to his thoughts.

"In 1931 the chapel was excavated by an archaeologist and a genealogist and, when they opened Vlad's tomb, it was empty except for animal bones – which only confirms my belief that he was never bloody well there, because he never died. The bastard is lying somewhere just waiting for the blood that will restore him – blood from the chalice. I have to do what I vowed I would never do. I have to find my maker – the First One – if he still lives. There are rumours that he allowed himself to perish at the turn of the millennium. I'm not even sure where to begin, only where he was last known."

"Where?" Lane asked.

Mihai's expression transformed as if hope had suddenly crossed his horizon. "New Orleans," he said.

CHAPTER SIXTEEN: THE TURNING

During the previous months, the one thing that had stood foremost in Mike's mind was the prevailing atmosphere of peace and tranquillity that pervaded Linwood House. It was the main reason he had agreed for his wife Beth to be sequestered there in a private apartment, tended by his trusted friend Beckett under the protection of The Strazca and primarily the head of that organisation, Roman Woolfe.

That peace and tranquillity had been abruptly pierced by screams of exquisite agony and mental anguish that had roared through the ancient timbers, elegant rooms, and corridors which were accustomed only to the quiet movement of the scholarly members of The Strazca, there to consult some ancient tome in the vast and comprehensive library. No thickness of ancient British oak door, or panelling, could contain the sound of such suffering.

He ran his fingers through his hair as he paced the sitting room, gracefully furnished in antique brocades and old leather. He was at a loss; out of his depth. Where the hell was Beckett? He had left Greece hours ago.

Mike had done everything that Beckett had instructed him. They had administered morphine mixed with a sedative but it had only bought them an hour or so. Darius was turning into a vampire and there was nothing he, or anyone else, could do to prevent it. In his lucid moments, Darius was aware of his condition, which only added to his mental torture. Mike had stayed with him through the worst of it, and now, as Darius slept fitfully under the influence of the drugs, he had left him in the care of Raven and Roman Woolfe. He needed to marshal his thoughts, quiet his agitation, and ready himself for the next phase of the turning; the most gruesome part of the entire process, when Darius was no longer fully human and would need to feed – on human blood.

Soft footfall on the plush carpet reclaimed his attention as Roman entered the sitting room. He didn't speak but moved silently to the Jacobean sideboard and poured two large glasses of brandy into beautiful crystal glasses that reflected the firelight as he passed. He handed one to Mike and, in mutual understanding, they sat in the armchairs facing the flickering, flaming logs in the fireplace.

Eventually, Mike broke the silence. "Can you honestly tell me, that with all your knowledge and resources, this is the first time you have seen this, or known of it? Honestly?"

Roman directed his attention onto the amber liquid in the fine crystal, as he swirled it carefully around the inside of the glass. He took a breath, and then said, "Honestly? Of course we have shelf upon shelf of old literature and folklore on the phenomenon, but nothing of recent origin, nor have I witnessed such a horror. The Strazca, as you know, is an organisation whose purpose is to observe and study occult phenomena – from a distance. Our remit is not to interfere or participate in any of the occurrences that may present themselves during the course of our studies. Until recently. You changed that, Mike."

Mike was appalled at the cold analysis of the whole situation. "*Me?*" he demanded. "Phenomenon? Remit? How can you sit there and talk like that, whilst that kid is suffering unimaginable pain, turning into … a … *vampire*? There, I said it … a vampire! *Jeesus*! You can be a cold bastard sometimes."

Roman appeared to be considering Mike's words. Then he said in a level tone, "But that's my job, Mike. The whole subject is emotive, it engenders a whole gamut of emotion – fear, belief, disbelief, misunderstanding and dare I say it, hatred? The ethos of The Strazca is to remove the emotion, to be impartial, objective observers and recorders of every occult phenomenon that we encounter, because how else can our studies be pure? Until you came to us, along with Ben and Jack, we had no interaction with any of it, no sense of justice or control; you did that. I have to say that it was with great reservation that we decided to allow it, but, as human beings, we found that – despite our best intentions – feelings did make themselves manifest. Now, with you to do the dirty work, we can once more detach ourselves from the 'sharp end' as you like to call it, and do our job *as* impartial, objective observers and recorders."

"But, what about the bloody arsenal you have in your basement – your precious 'artefacts'? Yes, some of them are religious objects, imbued with spiritual power, but you've got some heavy-duty weapons down there too? So, what the hell were you going to do with those, huh?"

"We knew a time would come when we could no longer stand back and watch some of the evil stalking this world. But we also knew that from the beginning we had taken an oath to remain impartial, because otherwise our research and study would not be pure. We are human, after all. Mike, I have to stand back and assess without emotion, so, yes, I am a cold bastard at times but that is because I can afford to be. Your job is to act on emotion and instinct and your infallible sense of right and wrong, to get your hands bloody while we keep ours clean. Right now, I have been able to detach myself from that poor boy's suffering so that I can mobilise our resources whilst we await theirs. And, if I am not mistaken, I hear the arrival of the car I sent to collect your friend from the airport. Which means your job is about to begin. Shall we?"

He indicated the open doorway, through which Mike saw Roman's assistant pass to open the front door. Heavy and purposeful footsteps accompanied by a lighter, more hurried, set brought Mike to his feet to greet his friend.

Beckett's face was set in a mask of unfulfilled fury and

Mike couldn't read his eyes. He put a firm hand on Beckett's shoulder. "I'm deeply sorry, Beckett. It all happened so quickly, we were lucky to get out alive. And I had no idea how to help him. We've done the best we could. I'll take you to him."

He turned to meet Lane for the first time and was taken aback by her casual beauty; he could read anger and hurt in her eyes too.

"You must be Lane; I am honoured to meet you at last, but we'll do the niceties later. Follow me; I'll take you to Darius."

Right on cue, a howl of pain rent the air. Beckett flinched and headed for the stairs, taking them two at a time, moving with vampire speed that Mike couldn't track. Lane was at the top of the staircase ahead of Beckett. Mike shook his head and followed at human pace.

Beckett had homed in on Darius's presence and was at his side, holding him against his chest, sensing for the phase of the turning. His face was even paler than usual as he realised that Darius had long past the point of no return in the process. Lane stood close, her hands helpless at her side as she too recognised that they were too late to prevent the turning. She wiped away a tear and Mike noted that it was blood-stained. Something new to ponder.

Beckett was talking softly to Darius, "I'm sorry, son. I let you down, but I promise you they will pay dearly. Blood from the House of Tepes is going to run."

Darius had a deathly pallor and Mike wondered how anyone could come back from such a condition. His thoughts were interrupted by a soft footfall; he knew the owner of the footsteps without turning around. Roman Woolfe had entered the room.

Roman stepped forwards to Beckett. "How can we help you? How can we help *him*? Our full resources are at your disposal. Just tell me and it's yours."

Beckett lowered Darius back onto the pillow and kissed the top of his head softly, allowing Lane to take his place.

He turned to Roman.

"Without the Sanctuary and its facilities and treatment administered immediately, there is nothing that could have been done other than what you have already done. For which I thank you. The turning is almost over; there is only one thing left now. He needs to feed. I will have to find a donor for him but, in the meantime, he will feed from me. I'll need a cup and a lancet, please. And some privacy; the first feeding is often shocking to witness."

Roman left the room as quietly as he had entered it, his face grave, but a light in his eyes that made Mike wonder about his motives. This was new to Roman and he was relishing the experience whilst genuinely offering his help.

A movement in the corner of the room caught their attention. Raven had been sitting quietly, allowing Beckett his moment with Darius. Now, she moved towards the bed and they could see the black streaks down her cheeks; she had been crying.

Darius lay back on the pillows, eyes closed and softly moaning. Beckett turned to Raven and she moved forwards and flung her arms around him. Beckett hugged her in return and then held her at arm's length, examining her closely. Since arriving at Linwood House she hadn't left Darius's side and there were still smuts and smoke smears around her eyes and on her cheeks. Raven was one of the longest-serving volunteers at the Sanctuary and Beckett knew her well; well enough to recognise the pain in her eyes and the loving glances that she continually cast towards Darius. He allowed himself a smile. So that was the lie of the land; Darius could do no better. A shadow fell over his face as the reality of their situation hit home. He hugged her again and felt the shudder run through her as she fought to contain her grief. He read her; something that he usually denied himself, but circumstances dictated the sharing of information. He needed to know everything.

Beckett led her gently away from the bed, casting a glance towards Darius, and, satisfied that he was resting between bouts of agonising pain and that Lane was right by his side, he drew Raven into the corridor.

"Raven, I need to know what happened. Everything, every detail, do you understand? I need to see what you saw."

She nodded. "You need to get inside my head; read my thoughts; share my memories. That means that you will know my every thought. I understand and I'll do it."

Beckett gave a half-smile, "It's okay. I know how you feel about him. I'll do my best to avoid those personal feelings, but it's vital that we know who is behind all this. I suspect it was Vasile Tepes and his thugs, but I need to be sure. You should know that this horror has been perpetrated in every Sanctuary across Europe and beyond. A war has begun; a war between the Born and the Created and we are going to need all the help we can obtain; vampire and human. It's going to be bloody and it may not end well for us. But we have to stand – stand together."

"Do it," she said.

Inside her thoughts, Beckett found his way easily to her memory of the fire. He could smell the acrid smoke and hear the alarms going off, he saw the young receptionist fall to the floor and the vampire thug fall on her and tear her apart. He heard the screams of the young man in the upstairs clinic room. Still he probed further, looking for a face to confirm his suspicions. Then he had it; the vampire who was feeding from the young receptionist's torn body, finally sated, stood and turned around. Even under the gore that clung around his mouth, Beckett recognised him – Constantin Tepes, one of Vasile's younger cousins, who had a reputation for his savagery but had never been brought to book by the Council. Vasile had always protected him, given him an alibi, but Beckett wasn't going to play by the rules now either. Now he knew where to start and he had the confirmation he needed; that Vasile Tepes was behind the new war.

He extricated his mind from Raven's and gave her a

hug. "Thank you, that was brave of you and generous. I'm so sorry you had to experience that at the Sanctuary, but I also want to thank you for being here for Darius." He smiled at her, and the smile reached his eyes. "I felt the love you have for him. Does he know?"

She shook her head. "No. He is always so busy and so serious; we have only ever exchanged a few words here and there. I would die if he rejected any suggestion of meeting away from the Sanctuary. I couldn't bear that."

Beckett's smile still hovered around his sensual mouth. "I should try if I were you. He may surprise you. Now, I have to go and find a donor for him. Will you stay with him?"

"Of course," she said, "but you don't have to find a donor; I want to do it."

Beckett frowned; there would be complications if she became his donor while there were unresolved emotions to get in the way.

"I know what you're thinking; that my role at the Sanctuary hasn't been one of a donor, but this is different. I love him, and – before you say that's a problem - it really isn't."

"Once he drinks your blood, he will know how you feel about him: it may complicate things. It's a huge commitment."

"I know what is expected of me, Beckett. It's what I want."

Beckett nodded and put his arm around her shoulders. "Let's get ready then."

CHAPTER SEVENTEEN: LUCY'S PENDANT

Vasile Tepes had complete control over Lucy's mind, and she followed him back to his sleek black limousine willingly. Her secret was secret no longer; her passion for the Gothic and all things vampire had only served to mask a darker yearning – to be one of them. Now she was going to see that longing fulfilled. She knew that Vasile was inside her head, reading her innermost desires and she could see from his expression that she fascinated him. There was no fear in her and that was seductive to him. He would enjoy her until she fascinated him no longer, and then he would dispose of her like so many of his other women.

He relinquished his hold on her mind as they arrived in front of his home, he had no need to control her; she was biddable because she believed he would make her a vampire. Perhaps she wouldn't be so if she knew that the very idea was abhorrent to him; that it was the very last thing that he would do; that Vasile Tepes was about to orchestrate the slaughter of thousands of Created vampires. He would let her believe in her fantasy for a while longer and, when he had tired of her, she would follow the rest of his lovers.

Inside his mountain retreat he bowed theatrically to her, laughing at her wide-eyed expression of appreciation of the plush rugs and tapestries, the wide sweeping staircase and the baronial fireplace alive with flaming logs; she had no idea that he was mocking her.

Whilst his home looked ancient, it was in fact fitted with everything for his comfort and the central heating system was discreet; the flaming fireplace was for his visual pleasure and not of a necessity.

He escorted her to a comfortable couch in front of the blaze and pulled on a tapestry bell-pull for Nicolae, who seemed to materialise in front of them from nowhere.

"Whilst you are my guest here, beautiful lady, Nicolae will see to your every need. When you want for anything just pull on one of these, there is one in every room."

Nicolae smiled at her and bowed his head briefly. There was no mockery in his gesture; he felt sorry for the girl, for it was certain that she had no idea of her forthcoming demise. It always ended that way. And it was he that always had to dispose of the bodies and any evidence of their presence.

Vasile was watching her closely, searching for any sign of anxiety or regret; there was none. She was fully aware of what he was and was relishing every moment – living inside a Gothic romance. He sensed the dark side of her nature surging to the fore and her delight as she began to realise her true self. There was no regret at leaving Dan with the others and whilst she had no knowledge of their fate, she didn't question what was going to happen to them.

As he trawled through her thoughts, he struggled to prevent himself from laughing aloud at her belief that she could hold the pendant over him as leverage for him to turn her. Foolish girl; he could take it at any time he desired. Deep down, he believed it was exactly what she wanted and he would take pleasure in playing rough when the time came. In the meantime he would use her to satisfy both of his hungers.

He instructed Nicolae to bring him absinthe and two crystal glasses. He would enchant her first, and he enjoyed his blood warm with a hint of the anise and wormwood.

They drank together and he entered her thoughts again, clouded as they were with the delirium of the neat alcohol laced with the hallucinogenic wormwood. He saw images of a happy childhood in the care of her grandparents and knowledge of the early death of her parents but no memory of it – they had obviously died when she was an infant. Her grandfather appeared in her stored images – a distinguished and educated man with silver hair and beard and a twinkle in his eye. As she thought of him, Vasile picked up a hint of sadness at his being away from home much of the time as he searched the world for artefacts and antiquities to add to his collection.

Images of her grandmother were very different – a spare woman with a lean and severe countenance who rarely smiled. She did her duty to the child and, in her own way, she loved her. But she was one of those women whose love was contained and measured with little display of affection.

Vasile probed deeper as Lucy fell into a deep sleep, unaware that he was raping her mind with no shred of remorse.

There was grief and tragedy as he encountered the memory of her grandfather's death and the subsequent selling off of his collection to enable her grandmother to keep their house. There was no money – he had spent everything in obtaining what her grandmother called 'his damned trinkets' and the sale of his collection barely covered the old man's discovered debts. Eventually, the house was mortgaged and Vasile sensed the change then in the old woman as she withdrew into her resentment until she too wasted away, a bitter old woman.

Vasile frowned. He probed harder, searching for memories of the pendant. He put the image into her mind, so that it would lead him to the archived memories.

He found it among the images of her late-teens. It was her eighteenth birthday and her grandmother had called Lucy to sit with her and had handed her a black velvet pouch.

"This is the last of it all," she had said, with bitterness that annihilated any affection – this was duty. She had continued in a thin, reedy voice, "He always told me that it was for you. He brought it home from a trip to Romania several years ago – the last trip before he died. He was never the same after that, fading away within weeks of his return. Doctors had no idea what was wrong with him – some kind of terminal anaemia, they said." She sighed. "Anyway, he told me that I was never to part with it and that you should have it when you came of age. Well, I suppose it's the modern thing now for that to happen on your eighteenth birthday. Personally, I think you are still a child, but I need to do this before … well, I need to give this to you now. It's your birthday present from your Grandpa."

Vasile watched her memory of slipping the pendant into her hand and he flinched at her innocence and delight, unappreciative as she was of the importance of the trinket in her hand. "It's beautiful!" she had declared. "Look, Grandma, it's a dragon and a goblet – and there's some strange writing on the back of it. Do you know what it says?"

Her grandmother had shaken her head. "No, of course not, and I don't believe that your grandfather did either. I have never opened the pouch since he gave it to me. It's yours now; do what you will with it." She had leaned back in her chair and closed her eyes then, effectively dismissing Lucy, who planted a soft kiss on the old woman's forehead before leaving her in peace. She had died that night, quietly and with no fuss, in her sleep – departing this world as she had lived in it, with little or no interest.

Vasile continued to probe Lucy's mind.

He watched as she had left her grandmother sleeping and rushed to her own bedroom, eager to fasten the pendant around her neck and admire it in her mirror. Vasile scowled – this was an insult to him as he witnessed her girlish joy in something of such import. He determined to dispose of her without too much delay; already he was losing his taste for her.

In her mental imagery, Vasile watched Lucy stop and

frown as she withdrew something else from the pouch – a folded piece of paper. She opened it up and gave a small gasp as she realised it was a letter from her grandfather.

My Dearest Lucy,

If you have been given this necklace by your grandmother, I am afraid, dear one, that I have passed from this life. I am stricken with some damn illness that no-one can define and am wasting away daily; some of the doctors think it may be related to two injuries on my neck that appear infected. Don't grieve for me, child, I have enjoyed every second of my life and have been fortunate to travel widely collecting what your grandmother calls my 'damned trinkets'. It is one of these that I am giving to you for your coming-of-age birthday. It doesn't have any priceless jewels in it, but it comes with something of a request. There is something very special about this trinket – something that requires you to take great care of it and allow it to pass into no other's hands. There are those who seek it, and for this reason it has been cut in half, way back in its history – perhaps even at its creation. I am told it contains a secret, though I know nothing of this, and that it must be kept in sacred trust. I have always loved this piece and leave it to you with my love.

Your ever-loving Grandpa.

Vasile's face took on a sneer. Foolish old man to believe that this would never come his way; it was his destiny to unite the two halves of the seal and retrieve Vlad's chalice, thereby restoring the House of Tepes to its former authority among his kind.

He took the pendant in his hand and tugged it roughly from around Lucy's throat. Two things happened at that moment – first, the image of its creator flashed across his mind - Mihai Rabinescu! And second, and more unexpectedly, he felt a sudden urge to kiss her.

She stirred and, before he understood why, she was in his arms and he was kissing her with a consuming passion that he neither welcomed nor understood. She was awake then, and returning his kisses. He pulled away from her and buried his face in her throat, his elongated canines piercing the flesh and finding a vein. He drank from her, savouring the hot saltiness of her blood, allowing it to fill his mouth as he pulled the life-force from her distended vein. She moaned softly, and appeared to swoon – a victim of the mind-probing, the absinth, and the sudden blood loss.

Suddenly he allowed her to fall back onto the couch and stood abruptly, wiping the traces of blood from around his mouth with the back of his hand with all the savagery of his inherent nature.

He strode to the fireplace, grabbing the crystal decanter of absinth and a crystal glass as he glanced back at her, passed out on the couch. She was murmuring softly as her hand sought the puncture wounds at her throat. Impatiently, he yanked on the bell-pull at the side of the massive, marble mantelpiece to summon Nicolae.

His servant materialised, rather than entered the room.

"Take her to the guest room, Nicolae. I will decide what to do with her later."

Nicolae murmured his comprehension and picked her up as though she were a small child – despite his advancing years he was possessed of incredible strength. He left the room as unobtrusively as he had entered it, leaving Vasile alone in his black mood and intended intoxication.

He carried Lucy into a bed-chamber adorned with ancient tapestries and beautiful hangings, and laid her gently onto a heavily-carved, oak four-poster bed. He pulled a brocade coverlet over her, murmuring, "May God help you, child."

CHAPTER EIGHTEEN: THE BAD HUNGER

Beckett had taken Raven into a small bedroom adjacent to the room where Darius lay tossing fitfully as the agony lessened and the hunger grew. Lane sat on the bed beside him, bathing his face and crooning reassuringly to him that it would all soon be over. She was glad his eyes were closed so that he couldn't see the blood-tears from her black eyes.

Since taking in the blood of the First Once via Mihai, she was changed. Her eyes, once a rich, dark brown were now coal-black, surround by fine red veins. Mihai had told her the red-veining would fade but she would always cry tears of blood. All her senses were enhanced and, following the sudden surge of ancient knowledge, her thoughts and inflow of information had settled and filtered. It was Mihai's blood that was taking precedence and she was glad of it.

Adopted into the powerful House of Medici in medieval Florence, the niece of Cossimo Medici and child-bride to his son Pietro, she had been made vampire six centuries previously and had seen the world develop, as science replaced alchemy. It was science that she was now pinning her hopes on to find a cure for vampirism, if there was such a thing.

Angry at herself for staying asleep in Greece for so long, and for leaving Beckett and Darius alone, she wanted to take full responsibility for what had happened. If she had been there … if Beckett hadn't kept his promise to her and left Darius while he waited and watched her wake … if … if … if! Her instincts were to feed Darius herself, but she knew that she was still in a weakened state and in any case, his first feeding, most certainly, should not be of a strain of the Blood of the First One. Even she knew that.

She had half expected Becket to do it, but on reflection she realised that once Darius was stable he would need a permanent donor and what lay ahead of them would require all of Beckett's strength.

Her thoughts were interrupted as Darius sat bolt-upright in bed, wide-eyed with realisation of what had happened to him, and the memory of the slaughter and fire at the Sanctuary brought a cry of anguish from him. He looked at her with such sorrow, she felt her vampire-heart would break and nothing would be the same ever again.

"I am so sorry, Lane. I failed you. I failed Beckett. Where is he? I can't bear the shame of it. He trusted me, and I let him down."

Before Lane could answer him, Beckett's voice made him spin around.

"You failed no-one, Son. No-one! Vasile Tepes and his foul crew will pay for this, and they will pay with their lives. The Born have declared war – a war that can only end in blood-shed and slaughter of the innocents. *I* am sorry – sorry that this has happened to you, that you have become this thing that will make you a target along with the rest of us, infant and ancient alike."

Darius slowly nodded his understanding. "It's okay, I thought I was going to die, instead I am become like you, and I will do my best to make you proud."

Beckett's voice broke as he said "You do that every day, Darius. I have always been proud of you."

A sudden spasm overtook Darius and he bent double, gasping at the pain. Another pain, this time in his mouth, twisted his face into a paroxysm of agony as his preternatural new canine teeth erupted, needle-sharp and elongated.

His face was a mask of fear that wrenched their guts and twisted their hearts; they were used to dealing with this on a daily basis, but this was different – this was Darius.

Lane held him to her and Beckett knelt at the side of the bed, fixing the boy's eyes with his own, holding him trance-like to calm him.

"Listen to me, Son. You need to feed. You need to feed or you will die. You know what has to happen, you have seen it often enough at the Sanctuary, and I have seen you soothe and calm others to whom this was happening. You have a donor. She is here and has already given as much of her blood as I dare take. It will be enough, but you will be hungry still. You must fight that hunger, the hunger that will come even after feeding, because that is the road that will turn you into a cold-blooded killer if you don't resist. You know all this, I have heard you explain it to many, but once the hunger takes hold you may lose sight of that. But we are here. No-one is going to leave you alone until it passes. Do you hear me?"

Darius had gone deathly pale, his pulse-rate had fallen to a faint and intermittent beat. They had to act swiftly or they would lose him. He opened his eyes as Beckett held the cup to his lips and allowed the first drops of Raven's blood to trickle into his mouth. He swallowed. Beckett allowed a slow stream of the red, life-giving fluid to fill his mouth. Darius gulped it down like a starving child.

His eyes were wide open, red-rimmed and red-veined as the blood surged in his veins. He gulped until the cup was empty, and then he opened his mouth, his teeth coated red, the canines glistening with the remains of the blood. "More," he said, "I need more."

Beckett pressed him gently back against the bed, shaking his head. "No, Darius. This is the bad hunger. You know this if you search your heart. You have fed, and you will need to feed again soon, but this is the hunger that you need to fight. Do you understand?"

Darius nodded slowly, his face almost translucent against the white pillow. "Help me," he whispered.

Lane had disappeared moments earlier and she

returned now with Roman Woolfe at her side. She held a syringe that was loaded with a sedative.

"This will help him fight it," she said.

Beckett allowed her to take over and administer the drug that would hopefully keep him sedated while the bad hunger wore off. He prayed it would.

Darius's eyes were half-closed and heavy-lidded in seconds; Lane had given him the limit. As he drifted into a quiet clam, he smiled as his consciousness merged with the blood. "Raven," he said, as he surrendered to the powerful opiate.

CHAPTER NINETEEN: A WORTHY COMPANION

Vasile Tepes was agitated. He was pacing his private sanctuary, pausing often to stare out of the massive picture window at the ruins of his ancestral home squatting on the crags on the opposite side of the valley at Poenari.

He made a sudden decision, threw the glass and remains of the absinth onto the floor and left the room with a grim expression and determined stride. Half-way across the vast landing he met Nicolae coming towards him.

"Sir, I have taken a telephone call from Alexis Vasilakis, he declined to be put through to you but simply bade me deliver a message: that the House of Vasilakis had considered your proposal and feel that they cannot support it at this time."

The principle of shooting the messenger was high on Nicolae's mind and he took a step backwards to await Vasile's wrath. The anticipated explosion didn't come; his master simply clenched his jaw, narrowed his eyes, nodded in silence and strode away towards the staircase leading to the underground crypt where Vlad lay awaiting his restoration.

The air down there was frigid and Vasile suppressed a shiver. Things were not going his way, which invariably meant that someone was about to have a bad day. He could almost feel Vlad's impatience and, for the first time in over a century, the ancient ruler was inside his head. *Do not fail me. Find my chalice and free me.* The implication that Vasile would not benefit if there should be much more of a delay was unspoken and unheard but, nevertheless, understood.

He cursed Alexis Vasilakis, knowing instinctively that, had the proposal come from Vlad, co-operation would have been instant. The resentment coiled inside him and his rage overtook him.

He took the stairs two at a time and threw open the door to Lucy's room with a crash. His desire for violence made it likely that she would be providing the outlet for it. She stirred as he entered the room and turned to him, opening her arms to him with a vulpine smile that shook him to the core. He stopped abruptly and stared at her. Momentarily, the thought passed through him that she would make an exceptional vampire. She was beautiful, possessed of arrogance that would match his own, with a hint of potential cruelty that he could only admire, and she had an underlying strength which challenged him. Yes, she would make a powerful vampire indeed, worthy of being his companion.

How could he think like that? How could he be tempted to break every commandment of his own making? It was unthinkable – abhorrent.

The rage that had welled inside him ebbed away as she got up and came towards him. His instincts now were to push her away, throw her out, get rid of her in any way he took a fancy to; after all he had the pendant.

Instead, he took her in his arms and kissed her.

The feelings that surged through Vasile were as unfamiliar as they were unwelcome; all his life, which had been considerably lengthy, his thoughts and actions had been governed by violence and an unassailable belief that his will was always to be obeyed. Now, in one day, this had twice been put into question.

First, Alexis Vasilakis had dared to challenge him and now this woman, who he could easily snap like a twig and cast aside, had put an idea into his head that would bring death to any other who dared think it. And yet, he could not deny the fascination that she held for him.

The situation was intolerable, and he let her fall to the

floor where she lay laughing quietly. He stood over her, part of him wanting to kill her instantly, to snuff out the life that was tormenting him; another part wanting to own her, possess her, make her into what she so obviously desired – a beautiful and powerful vampire.

Self-loathing and arrogance fought for supremacy. Arrogance was victorious. He was Vasile Tepes, head of the House of Tepes; he could do as he wanted, and he wanted her by his side, consort to his ruler. There had never been another that would compare. No-one would dare to challenge him on it and no-one would need to know that she wasn't of The Born. He was powerful enough to make others believe him. She had been the bearer of the pendant, therefore she was deserving of it.

These thoughts flashed through his brain at lightning speed and she appeared to sense his inner battle. She crawled towards him and stood in front of him, baring her throat to him.

"Do it!" she commanded. "Do it now. Make me live forever."

Something happened to Vasile Tepes then that he had previously foresworn. He fell in love – a savage parody of love that was governed by obsession, possession and violence.

CHAPTER TWENTY: THE BIG EASY

Mihai settled back into his seat on the long flight to New Orleans, grateful for the time to think. Vlad's chalice was missing, taken away by his own maker at the time of Vlad's death in 1476. He grimaced at the lie; deep inside he knew that Vlad was not dead and he suspected that Vasile Tepes, the present claimant to the throne of the House of Tepes and would-be ruler of the vampire race, had his ancestor's body hidden and ready for resurrection. The bloody chalice held the key to that and it was imperative that Vasile should not get his hands on it.

He dwelt on his part in the problem; on making the seal that could lead to its location, at the instruction of his maker. His thoughts went back to the time of his own making – his 'becoming'.

The year was 1107 BCE. Pharaoah Ramesses XI was weak and Egypt was ruled by the priests of Amun from Thebes. He had been taken to the temple of Amun as a scribe and had lived relatively well among the priests, until one day he was asked to deliver a papyrus to the High Priest, Ramose. Ramose was handsome, tall, and well-built, and some said he had been born of Seth – the evil God-brother of Osiris, one of the most powerful Gods of the Egyptians. Today, they would have said he was born of the Devil.

Mihai had been known as Hunefer back then, and had lived under the philosophy that to obtain a quiet and lengthy life it was advisable to do his job well, ask no questions, and obey orders to the letter. He had been aware of Ramose's reputation, but the High Priest had always treated him well, and he wondered how he had obtained such notoriety. It was on that fateful day that he discovered the truth.

He took the papyrus to Ramose's chamber immediately and, in his eagerness to please, he entered without waiting for permission. Ramose was kneeling over an inert body, drinking blood from the gushing vein in his victim's throat. He was startled by Hunefer's sudden presence and leaped to his feet. Hunefer was terrified and fixed to the spot, expecting at any moment to become Ramose's next meal.

Instead Ramose went softly to his side and bade him sit with him.

"Hunefer, you have seen what no other has seen. You have seen the reason they believe I am son of Seth – evil. It is because my years already number into the hundreds; I have served countless pharaohs of this land. But see ... do I not look as a young man? I was born a prince of this kingdom to a past pharaoh who was wed to his sister and was also born of his older sister. This lineage has caused my body to be something other than man. I am a man but I must feed as a hungry animal. Only you, Hunefer, know my secret, and because of this I have to be assured of your silence. I will give you a choice:- you may die at my hand at this hour, or you may become as I am. I have that power to pass on this living hell and have done so before now; sometimes by feeding and feeding my blood back to my victim, sometimes by birth. Several of my children have been afflicted as I am."

Mihai had made the choice willingly; to live many lifetimes in his beloved Egypt was a gift, not a curse, to him then, although he had often regretted his choice since, and he had soon become aware of the need to move from country to country. But Ramose had been kind to him, nurturing his infant vampire abilities, teaching him how to take the blood and remove the memory of it from his victim's mind. He taught him to read people, to place suggestion in their minds, to feed from them without killing them. He was his mentor and his friend.

But there were others – others that Ramose had made but been unable to control – others who fed and killed for the pleasure of it. And there were those that had been born vampire. And so it had continued down the millennia.

Mihai was one of the ancients, living for thousands of years, sleeping the Long Sleep, the deep vampire sleep, for centuries at a time, emerging with a new life, a new identity, moving from country to country to keep suspicion at bay. He had many wives and fathered many children, none of whom had been born vampire. But the Born continued to descend from the original line of Ramose.

He had met with Ramose over the millennia, knowing him as many names and living in many different places. Together, they saw to the rise and fall of the Roman Empire, saw plagues and civil wars of many nations – their paths crossing sometimes at random, sometimes in times of need.

The last time Mihai had contact with his maker had been in 1590, when he, under the name of William Smith, and Ramose, taking the name John Barlow, had been part of the company of John White, leaving England bound for the New World – America. Their mission was to establish contact with 115 men and women who had been left three years earlier as settlers on the island of Roanoake. On reaching Roanoake, the settlement was deserted with no sign of any pillage from neighbouring native tribes. It was simply deserted, with no clue as to what had befallen them.

William and John both knew that among their crew on that voyage had been two of the Born. To them, the mystery of the Lost Colony of Roanoake was no mystery.

They decided to break contact with one another and so Ramose, as John Barlowe, had remained in the New World, whilst Mihai, as William Smith, had returned to England.

Over successive centuries Mihai had occasional insights as to his maker's whereabouts until the last time that he had gone into the Long Sleep. At that time, Mihai believed he had lived in New Orleans as wealthy plantation owner, Vincent Baptiste. After that, no-one had seen or heard of him until the rumours of his demise began to spread. If the First One was still alive, this is where he had to begin his search.

He prayed it was so, for, without him, Mihai had no way of reclaiming and destroying the Blood Chalice, as it had now become known.

Hours later, he emerged from Louis Armstrong Airport into the bustling Louisiana city on the Mississippi River. Latterly labelled the 'Big Easy', it had become famous for its round-the-clock nightlife – ideal for anyone who was most wakeful at night and needing to feed. Over the centuries it had become a melting-pot of French, African and American cultures and religions, with Voodoo, Houdoo and Santeria at its heart. In short, New Orleans was the ideal city in which a vampire could live undetected for many years. He hoped that this was the case and optimism rode high – he had a name.

Several years previously Mihai had encountered another of the elder vampires – not quite an ancient as himself, but knocking on a bit in vampire terms. His name was Lafayette and he had been twenty-eight years old when he was made vampire, in 1806. Creole, born of a French mother and Haitian father in 1778 in Santo Domingo, Haiti, Lafayette was taken into slavery to a sugar plantation on the banks of the Mississippi outside New Orleans. It was there he was fed on and turned by one of his kind, long since disappeared from the pages of history, as insignificant a vampire as there ever was.

His and Lafayette's paths had crossed several times, and Mihai had taken an instant liking to, and trust in, Lafayette, whom he now hoped would help him to find his maker. Mihai's first call would be to Lafayette's voodoo store, Damballah House, on Bourbon Street in the French Quarter with its iconic wrought-iron balconies, close to the junction with Orleans Street. Damballah House was a small shop catering for tourists with the usual tourist voodoo tat, whilst behind it was the real store providing the authentic requirements for any genuine practitioners. It was also where Lafayette lived.

The bell behind the door tinkled as Mihai entered the store. A couple of young tourists were showing interest in mass-produced 'voodoo dolls' and handing over their holiday dollars to a young girl in traditional Creole dress, complete with long checked skirt over a white petticoat, white blouse, and turban – all for the benefit of the tourists, since she was born in Brooklyn.

Mihai waited patiently as they completed their purchases and smiled politely at them as they left the shop giggling.

He nodded to the young sales assistant and made deep eye-contact with her, sensing Lafayette's presence, "I'm looking for Lafayette, could you tell him I'm here, please."

Bead curtains at the rear of the store jingled pleasantly, giving entry to the coffee-coloured, shaven-headed vampire, resplendent in a bright tie-dyed t-shirt, jeans, and several strings of beads around his neck. True to his usual appearance, he had a cigar between his teeth and a glass of rum in his hand – the smoking ban in public places had little or no effect on Lafayette, who claimed that the room at the back of the public store was his living accommodation and the smoking ban could not be enforced.

He grinned widely behind the cigar, showing bright white teeth and revealing sharp, elongated canines that customers believed were for effect.

The sparkle in his vampire eyes assured Mihai of the genuine nature of the grin.

"Bonjou Mihai, ki sa pote ou nan pot mwen an?" He said, in Creole.

Greetings, Mihai, what brings you to my door?

"Se pou seye a beni ou." *May the Loa bless you.*

Mihai returned a warm smile and followed Lafayette

into the back room. "English, Lafayette, if you please. You know my Creole is lousy."

Lafayette laughed aloud, still gripping the cigar between his teeth. "So, what can I do for you, my friend? You haven't come looking for me for no reason? Unless it's bloodroot or cowrie shells? Or maybe a love potion from the recipes of Marie Laveau, huh? What are you searching for?" He laughed aloud again, apparently delighted at his own teasing.

"Not what, but who," Mihai replied. "I think you know who."

The smile faded from Lafayette's face, and he removed the cigar to swallow a belt of rum.

"Don't know who you're talking about, sorry."

"I think you do. Vincent Baptiste – if that's the name he's using still."

Lafayette shrugged and put down his glass. He shook his head. "He's dead – went into the Eternal Sleep at the turn of the millennia," he said, referring to the term vampires had for their death. "Figure he'd earned his rest. Now, join me in a glass of rum – no rubbish, only the good stuff for you, my friend."

Mihai shook his head. "No thanks. I heard the rumours but, you know, I've never been one to believe all I hear. I guess I'll have to look elsewhere."

Lafayette shrugged again, but this time his grin had returned and so had the cigar. "Please yourself, but you'll be disappointed. You sure I can't interest you in a love potion? Marie Laveau's best!" He burst into loud laughter again.

Mihai could easily have entered the younger vampire's mind, even though Lafayette's real age would give him some protection, but he didn't – not yet.

"I'll be staying at The Westin on the riverfront if you suddenly remember that he may not be in the Eternal Sleep."

Lafayette nodded, his grin absent – Mihai wasn't going

to give up on this and was obviously going to stick around.
He would have to be careful.

CHAPTER TWENTY-ONE: ROMAN'S SECRET

Darius settled into a quiet phase; the sedative that Lane had administered was doing its work, although no-one was under any illusion that it was temporary – very temporary.

Roman Woolfe lowered his voice, addressing Beckett and Lane. "You should come with me; I have something you should see. You should come too, Mike. I'm sure the young lady will be adequate company for him in his present state."

Beckett cast a glance at Darius and frowned; he could wake at any moment and surrender to the darker urges that would be surging through him. "I don't know … is it important?"

"I believe we have a problem in common – at least, perhaps a common solution to similar problems. Won't you come with me?"

Raven looked up from her chair at the side of Darius. "I'll be fine – just don't be long."

Lane took another syringe from her pocket. "If he … *needs* … this, just jab it wherever you can – for your own safety. I'll be back as soon as I can."

They followed Roman out of the room. Beckett's mood was black and Lane could feel the anger boiling inside him; she also knew that the rage was directed at what he saw as his own failings. She could sense the guilt building in him and sense his thoughts (which was something she tried endlessly not to do with Beckett): – he had failed Grace, he had failed Kat, and now he had failed Darius – failed those he loved. She knew also that there would be no talking to him yet – it would only make matters worse, if that was possible. Her own heart ached for Darius and for what was in front of him – what he had become and what he may yet become.

"This had better be good," Beckett muttered.

Mike was only a step behind Roman, wondering what it was that he wanted to share – surely he had seen everything at Linwood House that could be relevant. He was intrigued and more than a little concerned.

They followed Roman to the main hall and down the sweeping staircase to the basement, at the foot of which the interior décor had been continued, leading to a pair of huge oak doors.

On the other side they found themselves in a panelled ante-room where state-of- the-art technology had taken over and found its place. Roman stepped up to a retina scanner and placed his right hand, palm down, onto another scanner that was reading his fingerprints and the lines on his palm.

A buzzer sounded as a green light and digital readout '*Access Granted*' flashed on the security panel. The door in front of them slid open.

Beckett and Lane's reaction had been similar to Mike's when he had first followed Roman into the bowels of Linwood House – it seemed an eternity ago to him and he could hardly believe it was only two years ago.

Beckett gave a low whistle as he took in the unusual arsenal in front of him: rows of conventional weapons and ammunition alongside weapons that had obviously been modified. After all, the targets of most of these weapons were not human.

Together, Beckett and Lane sensed the provenance of other artefacts – Mother Theresa's rosary; bullets that held the energy of the crucifixion because they had been fashioned from the very nails that had punctured Christ's body; and, an arrow head that had the same source,

Roman walked on, pointing out various pieces of equipment and explaining their provenance. Beckett was becoming impatient.

"Couldn't this tour have waited? Darius needs us!"

Roman smiled at him. "I know, but please bear with me. You need to see this, I assure you."

They had reached the end of the armoury and they were faced with another set of security doors and scanners. Roman stepped up to the scanners and repeated the procedure, scanning his retinas and, this time, both hand prints.

The green readout flashed in time with the buzzer and the door opened as before. This time however, the contents of the room appeared to be contained in iron vessels of varying shape and size. Each container was carefully labelled.

"This is where we keep dangerous artefacts; things that shouldn't see the light of day. Anything that has the potential for pure evil is contained here. The outer room is our defence – this contains what Mike and his colleagues are fighting against. We contain them and study them in a safe environment. Now, here we are."

At the end of the room stood a bookcase containing ancient grimoires and other treatises and tomes on black magick and other dark aspects of the occult, including necromancy. Mike frowned – why weren't they in the library, with all the other ancient manuscripts?

Roman put his hand on a leather-bound copy of the *Munich Manual of Demonic Magic;* also known as *The Necromancer's Manual,* it was a 'recipe book' of a 15th century German magician for the evocations of demonic spirits. Roman acknowledged Mike's quizzical expression and laughed softly.

"Fake, Mike." He tilted the book towards him and a loud whirring noise came from behind the book-case as it slid to one side, revealing yet another high-tech doorway, where Roman had to perform the same ritual to gain access.

The steel doors opened with the soft whooshing sound and they stepped inside what was, in fact, an air-lock. The high-tech ritual of entry recurred and they found themselves in what appeared to be a hospital ward.

Mike was stunned – he was as shocked as Lane and Beckett and turned on Roman.

"What the hell …? Why have I never been here before? What in God's name are you keeping from me? What else is there?" He was furious and it was apparent in the volume and tone of his voice.

Roman held up a hand in an appeasing gesture. "I'm sorry, Mike. But you will see. It's very personal; I'm only sharing this with you now because … well, because I can't help wondering … well, you'll see. Come with me."

A white-coated doctor came up to them and greeted Roman warmly.

Roman took his hand. "How is she today, Kurt?"

Kurt Bauer spoke with a faint German accent. "She is peaceful – much the same." He smiled the physicians' smile – reassuring, but tempered with uncertainty – and extended his hand, inviting them to follow him.

In a room to the side they were faced with a plate glass window looking onto a beautiful young woman lying in a bed connected to a ventilator and a bank of machinery that would be at home in any intensive care unit anywhere in the world. On one side of her bed an army of syringes kept her constantly medicated and sedated, whilst an IV in her arm kept her nourished. Her luxuriant dark hair spilled over her pillow, framing her delicate features. A nurse in white scrubs was attending to one of the syringes.

Mike's anger dissolved into compassion.

Lane was first to speak, the doctor in her coming to the fore. "Who is she?"

There was an almost undetectable tremor in Roman's voice – *almost* undetectable. "She is my daughter; her name is Lowell and she is eighteen years old. She has been here like this for the last five years."

"What's wrong with her?" Mike asked softly.

"Ah, well now, in any other company I would say that

she had something that most people would understand – but to you, to you I will tell the truth. Lowell is a lycanthrope."

Mike took several moments to process the information, but Lane and Beckett were there the instant that Roman had finished speaking.

Lane moved closer to the glass window and leaned against it, her palms on the window. Beckett's hostility had completely vanished. "We have experienced this. There is a lycanthrope that we know of, living in Wales. He came to us for help, which we gave him to a certain extent, but unfortunately the help we gave him was limited and shamanic in nature – we were too late."

"Jude Mason," Lane whispered, her mind going back to the classically handsome ex-soldier and her friend, the Native American medicine-man, Jo Timberwolf. She was brought from her reverie by a barrage of questions from Beckett.

"Why is she like this? What happened to her? And what relevance does this have to Darius – he's vampire, not lycanthrope!"

Roman turned away, "Let's leave her in peace. Come with me and I'll explain."

Mike got there. "Lycanthrope? You mean …"

"A werewolf … yes." From Beckett.

"You know one? Living in Wales?" Mike was still processing.

Beckett put his hand on Mike's shoulder. "You have dealt with your ghosts, fallen angels and demons and, from what you tell me, you have met Lucifer himself. You know that I'm a vampire and so is Lane – and now Darius. Is it so much of a strain on your credulity?"

"No. No, it's not that. Just not what I expected. Wales? Really?"

They followed Roman into a comfortable sitting room, furnished with coffee machines and leather armchairs.

"This is the doctors' rest-room," he explained. "Please,

have a seat." He continued when they were all settled. "Lowell's condition is, I'm afraid, hereditary." He raised a hand at the alarm on Mike's face. "My name is no accident, it was given to my ancestors because of what they were – lycanthrope. Not all of them – it skips a generation or two every now and then. I am free of the condition but I choose to keep my name as a reminder of my duty to my family. When Lowell first showed signs of the condition I hired the best physicians I could find that had open minds and a yearning for research. I found Kurt in the Ludwig Maximillian University in Munich. He is a brilliant geneticist, and that too, it appears, is hereditary – though his ancestor did some terrible things with his talents. You asked me, what is the relevance? I heard you say that until now, you believed that the vampire condition was the result of a virus and that you had had some limited success with anti-virus serum. Now you believe it is genetic. Kurt is working on the principle that bad genes can be switched off. After all, Lowell, as with most lycanthropes – those that were born that way anyway – was perfectly normal until puberty or just after."

Lane was thoughtful. "Gene silencing," she said. "It's in its infancy."

Roman nodded. "Yes. But we must have hope. At the end of this corridor is the most up-to-date laboratory where Kurt works tirelessly to find the right gene and switch it off."

"In the meantime, you keep her in that state?" Mike was appalled.

Roman looked grave. "Oh yes. You see, the alternative is even more horrific."

He picked up a remote control and switched on a television and DVD player. Without warning, the screen was filled with a tortured face – a face that was neither human nor wolf. Gone was the sleeping beauty; instead was the howling beast.

"Oh God!" Mike exclaimed.

Before anyone could add anything further, Kurt appeared in the doorway, his face grave. "You should see this, Roman."

He took the remote control from Roman's hand and switched channels. On the screen were stills from security cameras. One screen showed Raven lying on the floor next to an empty bed. The second showed the open front door.

CHAPTER TWENTY-TWO: LAFAYETTE

Lafayette was thoughtful; his dilemma was simple – did he disobey his instructions from the First One – now known as Jean-Baptiste Vincent and 'living' in the affluent Garden District of New Orleans – and wake him from the Long Sleep? Or did he respond to Mihai's apparently urgent need to contact him?

Lafayette knew more of Mihai by reputation rather than personal contact, even though they had met occasionally, and his instincts told him that if Mihai said he needed Jean-Baptiste, he really did. On the other hand, Jean-Baptiste Vincent was the First One and common sense told Lafayette not to piss him off.

New Orleans had its fair share of vampires – most of them living peacefully alongside humans and feeding at the safe-house, New Orleans' 'Sanctuary', situated behind and under Mamma Beth's Bar and Grill on the edge of the Quarter, and some of them had even developed a taste for the blood of the alligators in the bayou – no accounting for taste in Lafayette's eyes – but there was a small minority that over-stepped the boundary, and then there were those who were just plain bad.

He pulled on the ever-present cigar and took a swig of rum. This was going to be a two-cigar-three-rum-problem. He was under no illusion that Mihai was going to be watching him, tracking him, and if he wasn't careful to cloak his mind as best he could, the ancient would be reading him.

Jean-Baptiste had been in the Long Sleep for years and had fostered the belief that he had in fact perished at the turn of the millennia. Lafayette had no idea why, but he had been chosen by the First One to guard his secret and his home and to care for his sleeping place. Lafayette was the only one to know his whereabouts.

Mihai hadn't told Lafayette why he needed Jean-Baptiste but, in his experience, when the ancients wanted a get-together there was some heavy shit going down. But if he questioned Mihai, it would reveal the fact that he knew something and wasn't saying – and that wouldn't be good for his health.

The end of the third rum gave him his answer – if in doubt, do nothing.

All of this had made him hungry. He had fed well only three days ago and his donor was out of town, so it would have to be the Sanctuary, after which he would bide a spell in Mamma Beth's, where the music was loud and cheerful and the company colourful. There was usually a parade of some description happening in the Quarter, and Lafayette wasted no opportunity to paint his face into the white, grinning skull of Baron Samedi and don his top hat. Tonight would be no exception, especially as he would be feeling in the mood after feeding.

He thought briefly of consulting the Loa – the voodoo spirits – for help, but dismissed it in favour of Plan A : the Sanctuary and Mamma Beth's.

Bourbon Street was buzzing, as it always was; a hive of activity of tourists, local shopkeepers and barkeepers, jazz bands and solo street performers. Lafayette adored it. Complete in the persona of Baron Samedi, he sauntered – no, swaggered – down Bourbon, into Orleans Street, past O'Briens and several jazz clubs, towards Royal.

Mamma Beth's wasn't going to disappoint; he could already hear the loud Cajun music and the laughter and noise of its feisty crowd – all of it adding to his hunger. He picked up his pace, unwilling to use his vampire abilities and almost materialise and draw attention to himself.

A few blocks from the safe-house, he was brought up abruptly by piercing screams and the acrid smell of smoke. People were running towards him in panic and out of the night came the sound of approaching sirens. He moved with vampire-speed then, rushing towards the burning bar, desperate to see if he could help.

Mamma Beth's was being evacuated and a fire-truck was just arriving to quell the flames; they would save the bar but, behind it and underneath, vampires lay slaughtered along with volunteers and donors – the New Orleans 'Sanctuary' was a blackened shell. There was nothing he could do for the murdered of his kind or any other that had been inside; all he could do now was to leave. As he did so, he caught sight of a vampire that he had met before: Constantin Tepes, a cousin and loyal thug of Vasile Tepes.

He ran to the riverfront and, reluctant to enter the foyer of The Westin dressed as he was, he took himself to the back of the building and began to ascend the fire-escape, all the while probing for an indication as to Mihai's location within. He found him on the top floor and entered through a window onto the corridor.

Mihai had sensed his approach, and opened the door of his suite and stood back. "Come in, Lafayette. I see we are both too late to stop this vile crusade, so I am guessing you have reconsidered my request?"

Lafayette nodded. "Yes," he said. "The war has come to our city and Jean-Baptiste will want to know about it."

"As I suspected, he is still alive. He is in the Long Sleep, I take it?"

Lafayette nodded miserably.

"Where is he? I think it better if I go alone, that way I can explain how I forced his location from you – and I could have – and you will be blameless in my disturbing him. Know this, there is more at stake than the war. An ancient evil is about to be brought back into play and I need Jean-Baptiste with me. If you want my advice, you'll get out of here and go far, far away. Take what you can and go, my friend; an ocean of blood of the Created is about to be spilled."

Lafayette appeared defiant at first but then, sensing Mihai's utter determination, he nodded his understanding and acceptance.

"He has a house in the Garden District. I'll show you."

They moved out of the Quarter at vampire speed towards the affluent Garden District, with its criss-crossing streets of colonial style houses, some large, some not so large, some brick-fronted, some stucco, all denoting wealth of yesterday and some of today. The streets were lined with avenues of crepe myrtle trees and Lafayette eventually stopped outside one of the larger homes on a corner plot. The garden was filled with camellias and other exotic flowering-shrubs. Wrap-around verandas on the ground floor, mirrored upstairs balconies and the windows were hung with heavy drapes, all of which were closed. The whole was well-maintained and Mihai couldn't help but wonder who was responsible for its upkeep; surely not Lafayette? But then, the tiny tourist-trap shop selling mass-produced voodoo tat on Bourbon would hardly support him so, yes, Lafayette had to be responsible. Mihai let it go.

Lafayette pulled a bunch of keys from his pocket and opened the heavy front door with an appropriately hefty key.

Inside, the house was in darkness and everywhere was still. Mihai could sense Lafayette's nervousness – it wasn't wise to wake a vampire from the Long Sleep, especially an ancient – but he dismissed it. He took several moments to appreciate the interior of the house in its faded beauty; everywhere was period furniture, carpets and drapes – a far cry from the monastery cell where Lane had laid in her deep vampire sleep.

"Where?" he demanded.

Lafayette nodded to the wide, sweeping staircase to the upper floor, but before he could reply, they both froze. The air was heavy with the scent of blood and death.

Mihai was at the top of the stairs before even Lafayette

could track his movement and, following the scent, he threw open a beautifully carved door.

The room reeked of violence: sprawled across the floor were two bodies whose death had been less than subtle — both of them had their throats ripped out with the savagery of a wild beast.

Jean-Baptiste Vincent was awake and feeding.

And he was gone.

CHAPTER TWENTY-THREE: DAVINA

Lucy's turning had surprised Vasile Tepes; it had been quiet and without incident. He could only assume that Lucy had been a Latent vampire – it was occasionally that way with Latents – and that technically, she wasn't one of the Created, despite his having turned her. It's what he told himself anyway.

He had been right in his appraisal of her, she was indeed, a stunning creature. Together they had left his mountain home and gone into the night to hunt their prey. It's how he liked it best – in the night, in the dark. Taking his food that way made him despise the Sanctuaries even more. This was how a vampire was supposed to feed – violently and from the vein – and not, as the Council would have it, almost apologetically and from simpering donors or, even worse, a plastic bag!

Lucy had found a savage side of herself that she previously would have spurned as she had gorged herself on her first victim and left him dead in a ravine. Vasile smiled as she took her second kill – a farm labourer living in a shack on the mountain-side. What a creature; he had made the right choice for his companion, and that night he had promised her everything – well, almost everything.

For now, he had cloaked his inner secrets; his sanctuary overlooking the ruins of his ancestral home and his ancestor, lying in the vault below them. One day, when he knew he had her absolute loyalty, he would share those secrets.

She was exhausted after her first night and was sleeping soundly as Vasile took her pendant into his sanctuary. Only half of the story it may be, but there was enough in it to tell him of its origins and its maker – Mihai Rabinescu.

Vasile's vampire gifts were honed to perfection and his skill in psychometry – the ability to read an object simply by touch – was impressive, even for a vampire.

He settled into his chair, the pendant clasped in his hand and his eyes closed, ready to delve deeper into the history of the seal.

He could 'see' its other half – a mirror image of what he held – making the image whole in his vision; two dragons facing away from each other and a chalice in the centre. It was a version of the seal of the Order of the Dragon.

He saw, in his vision, the Blood Chalice being removed from the fountain in Tirgoviste and the tall, lean vampire that had the audacity to do so – the First One. Only he would have had the temerity to challenge Vlad's authority. Well, he was dead and when Vlad was brought back by the power of the Blood Chalice there would be nobody to stand against the House of Tepes. Vlad would be grateful to him for his care over the centuries and for his search for the chalice – a search that was coming to an end; he could feel it.

Deeper into the pendant he went, watching images of its creation; Mihai was indeed a skilled craftsman. He 'saw' the seal finished and admired and then handed over to the monks at the monastery on Snagov Island by Mihai. And then he felt a sharp pain as he felt the seal being severed in two – and then darkness as the half he held lay in the grave next to Vlad's. He 'saw' the grave-goods excavated and taken to the museum in Bucharest. Then he watched as those artefacts were stolen and ended up on the black market where Lucy's grandfather had purchased the seal and had it made into the pendant that she had worn since her eighteenth birthday.

He went deeper still into the very metal, searching for its twin; searching for a clue as to its location. But it had been cloaked by the skills of the vampire who had ordered its creation – the First One. Only he would have the power to conceal it in this way from other vampires, especially one as skilled as Vasile.

He tried to contain his anger; it would only serve to block him. He opened his eyes as he became aware of Nicolae's soft footfall approaching. Moments later, there was a discreet knock on the door and his servant entered. He waited for Vasile to look up at him before speaking.

"Sir, you have a visitor. Shall I say you are away from home?"

Vasile frowned and then sensed the presence. "No, Nicolae, please tell my guest I will be with her directly."

Nicolae nodded and left in silence, leaving Vasile to curb his anger in preparation for a pleasant diversion. He sensed that Lucy was still sleeping soundly and so he could enjoy his visitor without complications. Nevertheless, he wasn't ready for Lucy's presence to be widely known and so he threw a veil over her room – one that would take extreme ability to penetrate.

Downstairs, in front of the massive old fireplace, Davina sat waiting for him. She had a glass of absinth in her hand and was curled up like a contented cat in front of the blazing fire; a second glass of the wormwood spirit stood on the side-table. Familiarity had made her pour the emerald liquid into two very old crystal goblets and settle back in comfort to wait for Vasile. She knew he would keep her waiting; the bastard always enjoyed making an entrance.

He approached her, arms open and a smile that hid nothing of his elongated canine teeth.

"Davina, I see you have made yourself at home. How pleasant to see you. I trust you took care of the matter at the hotel?"

"You know I did. Otherwise, you would not be so welcoming, Vasile. It was a shame about Christian, poor thing. He served his purpose, bringing the girl to my attention." She gave a cruel laugh. "At least he did it before I had to marry him. I trust you have what you wanted?"

Vasile smiled. "I have, thank you – at least, in part. To what do I owe the pleasure of your visit?" His manner was urbane, but Davina knew him well enough to know that underneath his demeanour was a ruthless and savage killer. It excited her and she smiled back at him, her eyes seductive and her movement feline.

"Do I need a reason? I thought we were friends, Vasile. More than friends."

She stood in front of him, a full glass of absinth in her hand, and offered it to him. He watched her from under heavy-lidded eyes as he took the proffered glass from her. She ran her tongue over her sharp, elongated teeth and put her hand around his neck to draw him to her, but stopped as she suddenly sensed his resistance. Davina was used to his mercurial moods and knew she would have to work harder to please him.

She lifted her wrist to her mouth and sank her sharp teeth into a vein, then held the wound over the glass of absinth, allowing the blood to flow into the spirit. But he was in no mood for subtlety. He grabbed her wrist and sucked hard on it, savouring the vampire blood freely given.

She waited for him to return the gesture, but it didn't happen. He let her arm drop to her side and sat in front of the fire, deliberately taking an armchair and not the couch which she had vacated.

She frowned momentarily, but persisted. After all, to be the chosen companion of the head of the House of Tepes was a goal worth working for, and Vasile Tepes had his eyes set on even bigger prospects.

She sat directly opposite him, aware that he was looking at her white neck and prominent vein, so she tilted her head slightly in order to distend the blood vessel into an offering. He had never refused it in the past. He leaned towards her, tempted to pierce the vein and drain her before leaving her corpse for Nicolae to dispose of. And then he had another thought.

She had been a faithful follower and useful into the bargain; she may still be such in the upcoming discussions with the other Houses – he had seen the way that Alexis Vasilakis had looked at her on the previous occasion and Davina was one asset that he wouldn't mind passing on now that he had Lucy.

Lucy – the thought of her entranced him. What was it that had drawn her to him in that way? Driven him to do what he censured and abhorred in others – to possess her and turn her?

As if he had conjured her, he sensed Lucy waking – sensed her rising and coming to him.

He had to act swiftly – Davina couldn't know about her; she would have believed he had used her and disposed of her, as was his usual practice, and as she was the only one who could recognise Lucy as once having been human, he would have to sacrifice her usefulness. He regretted the loss of an asset but he had to protect his position among the Born.

His eyes fell on the iron poker at the fireplace as he lifted her from the couch and pulled her close to him. She nuzzled his neck, happy in the belief that she had finally won him and, drunk on the absinth and his proximity, she remained unaware of his true intention until he thrust the poker through her rib-cage.

He let her fall to the floor and yanked on the bell-pull that summoned Nicolae, who appeared almost instantly.

"Get rid of that!" he snapped as he calmly climbed the stairs to his obsession – to Lucy.

CHAPTER TWENTY-FOUR: OF THE BLOOD

Nicolae cradled Davina in his arms, his loyalty to his master at breaking point as he looked down into the face of his granddaughter.

Countess times he had carried out Vasile's instructions without question but this time – this time it was different; this time it was family.

Instinctively, he pulled the poker from her chest with a loud sucking sound. Miraculously, it had missed her heart and Nicolae watched as her vampire body began to heal the terrible wound. He had to take her away from there before Vasile discovered his treachery, and to give her time to heal. His mind raced, searching for a solution.

Her eyes flickered open and she gasped as she sucked air in greedily. She caught his wrist and whispered, "Alexis. He will help me. Call him."

Possible scenarios flew through his head if Vasile discovered his secret and his actions – none of them ended well. He had been a trusted and faithful servant to the House of Tepes since he was a boy, when Vasile had taken him in as an orphan, giving him a home, a job, an income, and hope. But now he could see that coming to an end as all he wanted to do was to hold his granddaughter, take her away from there, away from Vasile who had no idea who she was.

"Hush," he whispered. "Hush. He thinks you're dead. I have to get you away from here.

He carried her outside and into the newly falling snow. It drifted around his head in tiny white specks that threatened to fulfil their potential and become large fluffy flakes which would quickly blanket the Carpathians in a white shroud. He glanced behind him but there was no sign of Vasile as he placed Davina in the back of the four-by-four and drove down the winding mountain road to the valley below.

The town of Curtea Des Arges, on the right bank of the Argeş River where it flows through the valley of the lower Carpathian mountains, came into view through the thickening snow. Nicolae pulled up outside the white-walled, iron-balconied hotel Casa Curtea and quickly carried Davina inside.

The receptionist was startled at the sight but was quickly calmed and sent away by the owner.

"Nicolae, you had better not have brought trouble to my door. I know I owe you, but this is asking a lot. Is he looking for her?"

Nicolae shook his head. "No. He believes her dead. It would be better for all of us if he continued to believe that. Please, just while she heals."

Alarm was immediately apparent on the owner's face. "Heals? Then she is vampyr? Nicolae … I dare not!" He crossed himself and turned away.

"Have you forgotten what I did for you? Have mercy, man – she is my granddaughter. Why else would I come to you? One night! Just one."

A cloud passed over the owner's face as the memory of his debt settled in his memory. He said nothing, but handed a key to Nicolae, who took it with a nod of gratitude.

"A quiet room at the back of the building. This clears my debt to you," Nicolae."

"This clears your debt to me."

Minutes later, in the quietest room in the hotel, Nicolae dialled a telephone number and waited for it to be answered in Greece. When it was, it was a surly voice at the other end who denied Nicolae a conversation with Alexis Vasilakis.

"Tell him that Davina Marinescu has need of him –

great need."

"Wait," came the curt reply.

Moments later a deep, rich voice, heavy with a Greek accent spoke. "This is Alexis Vasilakis. Who is this?"

"My name is Nicolae Marinescu, sir. You have made my acquaintance in the house of Vasile Tepes, though, as his manservant, I doubt you would have noticed me."

"I remember you. What do you want of me?"

"I called you because I was asked to by my granddaughter, Davina Marinescu, whom I believe you have met on several occasions in the company of my employer. He has turned on her and left her for dead and instructed me to dispose of her body, but I have her safe – for now. If he finds out I have her, he will kill us both. My granddaughter asked for your help with her last breath before she fell asleep to heal. Please, help her."

There was momentary silence at the other end, and then, "Where are you? I will send someone to you at once. When he arrives you can leave Davina safely in his hands. She will be brought to me, here in Greece. You know I have the resources. So, be assured you can trust me. In the meantime, I ask you to return to Vasile's home and act as though you have carried out his instructions. Tell me – Davina, is she … of the Born?"

"Yes, and – before you ask me – no, I am not vampire. But there have been several in our lineage. My wife was 'of the blood' as you say. And my daughter. I neither know nor care how the genetics work, only that my granddaughter is safe. I thank you for that. I also know of Vasile's forthcoming plans for another war and will be thankful if she is out of the way."

"Stay with her, someone will be with you soon. I have a great many contacts in Tepes territory."

Nicolae was satisfied. He believed Alexis Vasilakis, if for no other reason than he had seen the way Alexis had looked at Davina the last time they were together and also there had been an ill-concealed resentment of the head of the House of Tepes.

"I have her in Curtea Des Arges – a small hotel just on the outskirts, alongside the river – Casa Curtea. Room eighteen at the rear of the building. I would ask that whoever you send, comes quickly."

He was answered by the distant click of a disconnected call.

CHAPTER TWENTY-FIVE: HUNGER AND HUNTING

Beckett was out of the front door and into the darkness – Darius was nowhere.

Lane and Roman had gone straight to Raven, and Lane had lifted her effortlessly onto the bed. She woke with a start.

"Darius!"

"It's okay, you're okay," Lane soothed.

Raven's hand went gingerly to her head where there was the beginnings of an impressive lump. "It happened so quickly," she said. "He was sleeping soundly, and then he sat up all of a sudden and went wild. I tried to grab him but fell in the process. I banged my head on the way down – he didn't attack me, honestly."

Beckett returned, his face set in a mask of fury that was largely aimed at himself. Lane read him from a mile off.

"Easy, Handsome. None of us could have foreseen this. I gave him enough sedative to knock out two horses for a whole day. I can only assume that his strength and rapid assimilation of his vampire traits means that, somehow, Darius was bitten and turned by a very powerful one of our kind."

"Who?" Raven asked.

Beckett spoke through gritted teeth and it came out almost as a snarl. "I don't know, but I'm willing to bet Vasile Tepes was behind it – behind everything. He just keeps adding to my list of scores to settle with him."

Lane frowned. "He may have orchestrated it, but I would have sensed him if he was here. My instincts tell me he's still in Transylvania."

Beckett made a derisive sound. "Of course he is – he

won't get his hands dirty until he has to."

He was interrupted by his phone ringing in his pocket. He grabbed it and jabbed the answer button."

"Beckett," he snarled.

"It's Helena," said the soft voice at the other end. "Mihai told me about the Sanctuary – and my lab. He said I should come to you. Is everything all right?"

He put the call on speaker and gave her the abridged version of events but his tone was enough to paint a fuller picture.

"I'm on my way from Glen Lyon in Scotland. I … I'll tell you more when I get to you, but Lane is right … this is genetic and if we are to come up with any cure, I need to find the right gene."

Roman nodded in answer to Beckett's unspoken question.

"Come to Linwood House – I'll send you directions. I believe we have found you a new lab."

"And Darius?" she asked. "It's going to be too late to try the old serum on him, even if I could get any in a hurry."

Beckett struggled with his emotions that were flying between anger, frustration and extreme anxiety over Darius. "I'm afraid you're right, he's gone and we're about to go looking for him. Drive safe." He cut off the call and made for the door with Lane and Raven right behind him.

*

Darius's senses were on fire; he had never felt so alive. Everything was sharp and magnified a thousand times. His instinct to hunt was driving him wild and he had had no option but to leave. If he stayed he feared what he may have done to Raven – to any of them. He was hearing sounds from a distance – a couple making love; another couple arguing; a child crying; an old woman dying – sounds that merged in his brain in a cacophony of noise.

He could smell the scent of fallen leaves, of newly turned earth and all manner of human scents. But most of all he was hungry – and he knew he had to feed in the most primal way for a vampire – from a vein.

He ran through the darkness towards the village of Alderley, exhilarated by the speed with which he could travel, feeling the wind rushing through his hair and the blood pounding in his veins. His need to feed was greater than the instinct for survival and he knew that to satisfy his hunger he would have to disappoint Beckett. He didn't know where this force was originating and he couldn't afford the luxury of dwelling on it, though he knew deep down, that if he took the blood by force he would become what he had previously hunted. Was he to become like his brother, Andrei, had been?

The village appeared in a couple of minutes under his newly acquired speed and he wasted no time in obtaining a car – vampire speed alone wouldn't put enough distance between him and Beckett and the last thing he wanted was for Beckett to witness what Darius knew to be inevitable.

He was driven by an insatiable hunger that was becoming an exquisite agony, but he wanted miles between him and the others and he knew he needed clothes to replace the scrubs he was still wearing. A customised motor-cycle in the driveway of a house made him pause and smile. The rear window gave under his strength without too much noise, and he was in the house and up the stairs with newly-found lightning speed. Inside the bedroom, the owner of the bike was sound asleep in the arms of a reefer, and his discarded tight, black leather pants and jacket were a temptation too big to leave. Darius had a new look.

A small, run-down cottage on the edge of the village showed no lights, but Darius's night-vision was honing in on a small car in the driveway. He felt the bonnet – still warm – its owner was probably still awake.

He listened to the sounds of the night and then he

suddenly took a step back.

He could hear a woman inside the cottage, whimpering and pleading, then the sound of heavy breathing and the dreadful sound of something hard coming into contact violently with soft flesh. The woman cried out. The sound came again, this time accompanied by expletives and a warning to shut her mouth. The sound of flesh taking a beating came again and now he could smell blood.

He kicked out at the cottage door and was upstairs before any human eye could have followed his movements.

She lay in a heap on a dirty mattress, covered in her own blood that was slicked over old wounds and bruises and Darius could sense her approaching death; could hear her heart struggling to survive. The brute stood over her, his fists coated in her blood, a look of surprise on his face at the young man that had suddenly appeared before him. He growled and balled his fists, lunging towards Darius who met him head on, canine teeth down and looking for a vein. He pushed the man backwards against the wall as if he had been flicking a feather, but the man went back with enough force to knock the wind from him. His expression changed from one of surprise to one of terror as Darius attacked him with full force, tearing flesh from his neck with his elongated, sharp teeth and drinking the fountain of blood that gushed from the severed blood vessels. He pushed the man back against the wall hard and drank his fill, gorged on him, sensing the man's terrible crimes, seeing the faces of the women he had raped and killed. He drank the rest, feeling the heart losing strength as he sucked the life-blood from the murderer in his grip. He drank the last of it and allowed the body to fall onto the floor, empty, before rifling through his pockets for the car keys.

Bending over the woman he brushed the straggly hair away from her bruised face and looked down on her, feeling a pain so deep it made him weep. He picked her up, filthy blanket and all and carried her out to the car, where he laid her on the back seat and covered her with the blanket.

He drove to the nearest town, conscious of her stirring; trying to speak.

"Hush, now. You're all right; he can't hurt you anymore. I'm taking you to where you can get help. Don't try to talk."

His voice was soft and reassuring and she settled back against the seat as he drove to the hospital. Once there, he lifted her gently from the car and moved with such speed, no-one even saw him enter the building. He laid her on a trolley, bent and kissed her forehead and left the same way as he had entered.

He was wired; full of blood coursing through him, tasting the fear and the death of the man who had, all through his mean, miserable life, done nothing but inflict it. He wondered if he should be feeling remorse; he had, after all, just killed a man, whether or not the bastard had it coming. He didn't – he couldn't. He drove faster towards the motorway that would take him home – knowing only that it was where he felt safe.

Then the hunger overcame him and the pain that accompanied it was unbearable. He cried out in torment; cried out for Beckett, for Lane, for salvation. He drove it into a tiny village just off the motorway as the dawn was breaking and headed for the square tower of the village church. Sanctuary. They had to give him sanctuary, didn't they?

But the church was locked. In despair, he slumped against a tilted gravestone and wept.

CHAPTER TWENTY-SIX: UNSETTLED OLD SCORES

Vasile Tepes had been correct in his assumption that Lucy would make a beautiful and stunning vampire; in truth, she had surpassed all his expectations. Her breath-taking beauty was eclipsed only by the emergence of her darker nature that had previously been held in check by her humanity. Nothing of that remained now, and in the ascendancy was her instantaneous understanding and embrace of her new abilities. Vasile was entranced.

She matched him in strength and cold savagery during the kill, and her lust for the crimson liquor of life seemed unquenchable in these early days. So much like him. But he was also aware that he had to keep her old humanity a secret. How could he gain the co-operation of the other houses of the Born if he were to be found having not only to have turned her, but had allowed her to live – everything that was contrary to his loud protestations that all the Created were nothing more than vermin to be exterminated.

He stroked her hair and pulled her to him. Her kiss was so much more than the mere touching of lips – it held promise of something deeper and darker and he knew that mere love-making would not even come close to satisfying his hunger for her. He made a decision. He would tell her everything – show her everything. He wanted her at his side in what was coming and he knew that she would demand no less.

"There is someone I want you to meet," he said.

Lucy followed him down the sweeping staircase and further down to the crypt below them. A slight frisson erupted on her pale and translucent skin. She sensed him

141

lying there – waiting.

Vasile turned on the light and she was almost disappointed that the light had not come from a flaming brand on the wall. He 'heard' her thought and smiled – maybe there was a whisper of her old humanity there after all.

Lucy was looking around the crypt and back again to the desiccated body of Vlad, lying in wait for the sustenance from the chalice that would wake him from the Long Sleep – long enough to almost be the Eternal Sleep.

"I know who he is," she said. "Your ancestor – Vlad."

"My great-grandfather."

"I would like my pendant back now, please. I know why you took it and I know what he wants. The chalice. You must know this – you gave me your blood, Vasile."

He nodded. "Yes. I knew the consequences."

"But I also know where the other half of my pendant is. Here, in the presence of Vlad, take my blood again and see for yourself."

She offered him her wrist, which he brushed away, reaching instead for her neck. "The old way," he said.

Her blood coursed through him, making him immediately aware of her incredible power. How could this be? She was Created and not of the Born, and yet her powers of psychometry and her ability to read even him, were amazing. He would need to be cautious.

He allowed his mind to be filled with what she had seen.

He was 'inside' the chapel on Snagov island and looking down onto the grave of a monk. He focussed his attention on her blood again and now the image of the skeletal hand clutching the other half of Lucy's pendant became sharp.

"Snagov," he said. "I'm leaving now."

"And I'm coming with you," she replied.

He was momentarily annoyed, and then softened as he realised that she was going to be an asset not a threat.

When he brought the rest of the Born to heel, she would make a fine consort as he took control.

*

Vampires flying through the air is pure Hollywood; effective but not accurate. They do, however, have incredible speed and also incredible networks that they call upon at a moment's notice. It wasn't just the High Council that had their own pilots and airplanes, and Alexis Vasilakis as head of the House of Vasilakis had command of such resources. And so, just two and a half hours after he had spoken to Nicolae, Davina, in the healing stage of the Long Sleep, had been carried from the private jet into a waiting limousine to take her to Alexis's expansive home in Athens with its breath-taking view of the Parthenon. Alexis was in control of old money – very old money.

He looked down at her sleeping and brushed a stray hair from her forehead, then he carefully revealed the wound in her chest – it had begun to heal well. Rage bubbled inside him at her treatment at the hands of Vasile Tepes and old scores unsettled now claimed priority attention. Vasile wanted his support in the seemingly inevitable war which was now no longer an option. He wanted a war – he would get one.

Davina stirred and mumbled something incoherent. This was nothing unusual in this happening during the Long Sleep as the sleeper experienced visions and information from multiple vampire sources.

"Shh," he whispered. "Rest, Davina. I will take care of you." *And him,* he thought. *Time to involve the Ancients. Time to make a stand.*

She still appeared troubled and her wound had ceased to heal. She suddenly cried out and tried to sit up.

"Davina, it's Alexis. You're safe, you need to sleep and heal."

She shook her head. "Not yet," she managed in a

hoarse whisper. "Listen. Vasile has turned her. He's taken her for his consort and turned her."

Alexis was stunned. "Who?"

"The English woman. He took her and he turned her and he is keeping her in his lair."

Alexis smiled at her. "You know this because you have seen it in the visions of the Long Sleep?"

"Yes. And I saw something else, though I don't know what it means. There is a chalice and there is a crypt below Vasile's home where one of our kind is waiting. Vasile is going to Snagov."

Alexis knew its meaning; he had long suspected that the body of Vlad had never been at Snagov and every vampire House knew of the legend of the Blood Chalice, but remained complacent in the belief that it would never be found. Could it really be that Vasile Tepes was going to dare to restore Vlad by feeding him from the Blood Chalice? He dare not think of such consequences. There would certainly be a war then, and none of the other Houses would be able to stand up to Vlad. They never had. He leaned in close to Davina.

"Are you sure?"

She could only manage a small nod of confirmation before falling into the deep sleep of healing, her face portraying peace now she had managed to tell what she had seen to Alexis. She felt his admiration for her and she knew she had come home, however far from her birthplace that might be.

Alexis covered her with an antique quilt and bent to kiss her before leaving the room with grim determination written on every pore. Vasile Tepes, the great reformer, the one who wanted to exterminate all of the Created as abominations, had done what he preached against because it suited him. His supreme arrogance at previous gatherings, where it had been obvious to every other vampire present that his ultimate intention was the subordination of all to the House of Tepes, with himself at the Head, had sickened Alexis. And Vlad? He shook his head. Not going to happen. Some dead vampires needed to stay dead. He had to act fast – had to find the chalice before Vasile.

CHAPTER TWENTY-SEVEN: ON THE BAYOU

New Orleans is a city of the night, coming to life after sunset. Jazz music fills the streets and bars and the nightlife is focussed on the darker side of human and not-so-human nature. It's a haven for vampires where they can feed on the constant stream of tourists, satisfying their hunger but leaving them intact. Most of those that provided such sustenance relished the fact. Easy pickings, so it seemed.

Lafayette and Mihai combed the French Quarter, searching for traces of Jean-Baptiste Vincent – the oldest living vampire – now gone rogue if their eyes told them the truth.

"What are you going to do if we find him?" Lafayette was in no mood for taking on the Ancient of Ancients – the First One.

Mihai shook his head; he hadn't thought past finding his maker, his mentor. Now it seemed as if they would meet on opposite sides. It hurt. But Mihai was the Patriarch of the Council and he could not forgive such callous slaughter as he had seen in Jean-Baptiste's home. If it came to it, he would kill his maker personally. But first he needed the power of the First One.

Like any large city, New Orleans had its teeming underbelly. This was likely to be Jean-Baptiste's feeding ground – and he was going to be hungry if, as was now apparent, he had been in the Long Sleep since the turn of the millennium. It was also Lafayette's city and Mihai was happy to follow his lead out of the city, towards the bayous, away from the tourist trails, and into the deeper, darker waters cloaked in moss-draped cypress trees, trailing

147

their tendrils into alligator-infested swamp. Out of the city and on the banks of the Mississippi, Lafayette struck a deal to hire a boat, speaking in Creole with one of the only humans locally to have any truck with the vampires of the Big Easy.

Mihai boarded the boat that should have been condemned a decade ago with a reluctance that gave Lafayette great amusement. After a couple of wheezy coughs, the motor chugged into life and they left the shore and crossed the river to the brackish backwater.

Occasional houseboats gave way to Louisiana wildlife, mainly of the alligator variety. Suddenly, around a bend, a floating shack came into view and Lafayette steered the boat towards its jetty and pontoon.

A Creole woman in full traditional dress of long, layered check skirts and turban, worn out of love not commercial motive, appeared in the doorway. She looked like a rare exotic bird as she leaned against the door jamb and puffed heavily on a large cigar She eyed Mihai disparagingly.

"So, Lafayette, you bring another blood-drinker to my door. You had better have good reason, child."

Lafayette grinned at her and greeted her in Creole. "Bonjour, Monique. Koman ou ye?"

She gave a deep throaty laugh as she answered him. "I'm well, child. How is it with you? And more importantly, what do you want? Something to do with the blood-drinker that has just woken?" She laughed again at his look of surprise. "What? You are surprised the old voodoo queen knows what's on your mind? Come on in and sit a spell, while I throw the bones. You want to know where he is? I can tell you, but it will cost you a bottle of rum."

"It's yours."

She moved, cat-like, all hips and shoulders, into the dark interior of the cabin on the bayou. Once inside she indicated a sofa set against the wall, in front of which was her voodoo altar. Mihai remained impassive but Lafayette was obviously impressed by the tiers of candles, photos and statues of various saints, a human skull, an alligator skull, bones, sticks and beads, but most of all, candles. All were lit as if waiting for their request to be heard by the saints and Gods. Monique puffed hard on her cigar until it blazed in the dim interior of the cabin, and lit some charcoal from the bright ember. She threw on some incense and began moving in a circular motion in front of the altar, faster and faster until Mihai thought she would fall in a faint at his feet.

Eventually she stopped, her eyes glazed, and collected the bones and shells from her altar. Without ceremony except for the muttering of what sounded like a curse, or failing that, someone had better look over their shoulder, she threw the bones and shells onto the floor. She knelt in front of them and stared at them for several minutes, all the while muttering under her breath, and then sucked air in loudly between her teeth that still clutched the smouldering cigar.

"Many are converging on the prize you seek. The ancient blood-drinker is ahead of you and so is the enemy. Much blood will be spilled if he is allowed to steal the prize. The awakening of something ancient and evil will follow. But there is one who is young in the blood that will decide the outcome. Your destination lies across the ocean to where your enemy lays waiting. He is impatient and that which you seek was hidden where it was once proudly displayed."

"At the fountain?"

Monique shrugged. "That is all the bones will tell me. The rest is up to you."

Mihai made an impatient noise and stood abruptly. Monique scowled at him.

"Lafayette, you should teach your friend some manners. He needs to learn to respect the Loa of this place, or maybe they will teach him themselves."

Lafayette stood and hugged Monique. "Forgive him, Monique. I thank you and the Loa on his behalf and your bottle of rum will be with you as soon as I can arrange it."

She flashed a grin at him. "None of the tourist crap. Monique should have the best."

He grinned back at her. "Consider it done. I would never insult you with the tourist rum. I value my skin too much."

Mihai was already in the boat as Lafayette took his leave of Monique, and when he reappeared at the jetty, he spoke impatiently.

"We have no time to waste. We need to get to the airport as soon as possible."

Lafayette frowned. "We? There's a whole lot of '*we*' in that statement. Do I get a say in this?"

Mihai raised an eyebrow. "Of course. If you wish to assist in saving our kind then come; if not, then stay in this place and wait for the Born to descend and wipe you out. I can't think they will take kindly to knowing your part in this so far."

Lafayette tipped back his head and let out a booming laugh, his white teeth flashing in the falling gloom. "You are very persuasive, Patriarch. I see my choice is no choice at all. You have a reputation of being a bastard and I see it is accurate. Where are we going?"

"Transylvania."

CHAPTER TWENTY-EIGHT: SLEEP

Beckett was beside himself, using all his vampire powers to try and track his beloved Darius. The boy was out of control and he should have seen it coming. He should have stayed with him despite all the curiosity about Roman Wolfe's underground facility. He should have ... should have, should have. The scenarios were endless and he had allowed his 'adopted' son to fall prey to instincts that he had to control or become irretrievable.

He was mollified, only slightly, by the fact that Darius had slaughtered and fed on one of humanity's vilest criminals. One who would never be mourned, never be searched for, and would never again prey on and torture life's innocents. But that didn't mean Darius wouldn't succumb to the most predatory of instincts in a newly-turned vampire and gorge on the blood of an innocent. He wouldn't be able to defend or protect him then from the fullest weight of the Council.

Lane was tight-lipped as she too closed her eyes to overlook Darius and locate him.

Both of them saw the bloodied, yet bloodless, remains of the man who had left the young child that he had just abused hunched in a corner, with nothing but terror etched on her tiny face and a blank stare in her eyes. It wasn't far away and Lane left immediately to reach the child and erase her memory of the ordeal, or ordeals, that she had survived. She cleaned up the scene and put the child back into her bed, heavily under Lane's influence, where she would sleep the sleep of the innocent for the first time in years. There was no trace of the incident or the man remaining when Lane left, and he would simply have disappeared. At least Darius was homing in on the unspeakable to feed, but that held its own dangers. If he continued to consume the blood of these filthy beings, it would taint him. She or Beckett had to find him before it was too late – before there was no going back.

Beckett was calling to him across the ether, searching, tracking, and then suddenly he saw him.

Dawn was breaking on the horizon and mist was crawling across the ground at ankle height around the gravestones. The Norman tower stood veiled against the rising dawn and Darius had tried to enter the sanctuary of the church, but found it locked against him. The hunger had robbed him of his new strength and he was huddled against a gravestone that was leaning to one side, his knees pulled up against the morning cold. Beckett 'scanned' the outside of the church and his mind settled on the noticeboard at the old lych-gate – St Mary Magdalene, Tormarton.

He knew it. It was a small village just off the M4 motorway about an hour away from them, but he knew Lane would drive without care for speed limits so perhaps forty minutes. He prayed that Darius would stay hidden.

They barely spoke as they sped towards Darius. Beckett tried to keep his 'hold' on him though communication had broken, but he could still 'see' him hunched against the cold granite.

Thirty minutes past. Thirty-five. Forty – and the church tower drew them in.

Beckett leaped from the car leaving the door open wide and Lane was right behind him. He spoke softly, responding to the desperate look in the young man's eyes. "Darius?"

Lane stood away, on the alert and ready to ward off any intruders on the scene, as Beckett lifted Darius effortlessly into his arms and headed towards the car. He sensed the rabid hunger, the blood-lust, rising – and the panic inside. There was only one way to dispel it.

He opened a vein in his own wrist with practiced ease

and held it towards Darius.

"Drink," he said, "and then sleep. We are taking you home."

Lane flashed a warning glance at him and he read her. They weren't going home – they were heading back to the Strazca headquarters, to Roman Wolfe and to sanctuary. He nodded his understanding to her, picturing Darius sleeping in the next room to Roman Woolfe's daughter, Lowell, subdued by the same cocktail of drugs that held the beast in her in check, at least until they could round up enough donated blood to keep him fed and his ravening hunger at bay.

*

Mike Travis waited for his friend, Beckett, at his wife's side. She was still lost in her own world – a world where no demons existed and hell was a place in the imagination of ancient clerics. He read to her for a while, until she drifted into a contented sleep populated only by pleasant dreams. He watched her for a while and then, unable to keep his thoughts positive, he went in search of Roman.

He had only been part of the Strazca for a short while, during which time he had been hunting minor and not-so-minor, demons whilst studying in the vast library on the first floor of Linwood House, the Strazca headquarters owned by Roman Woolfe, the head of the organisation. His old friend, Martha Treneglos, served there as librarian, but he shunned the usual peace of the library and went in search of Roman. The man had many questions to answer and Mike was angry.

He found Roman in his ground-floor study and entered without knocking.

"So, when were you going to tell me about her? What else have you kept from me? I think I have earned your trust, for God's sake! What other secrets are you keeping? I mean, I have practically lived here for the past six months and only now do I find out about the underground facility where your daughter is lying in a drug-induced coma to keep lycanthropy at bay!"

Roman stood up and indicated for Mike to sit down. Mike ignored the invitation.

"I know how you must feel, Mike …"

"*Do you?*" interrupted Mike. "Do you *really*? I feel like maybe I don't belong here after all."

Roman's face expressed his genuine distress. "I'm so sorry, Mike. I really am. It's just that with Lowell, it's so raw, even after all this time. She is so beautiful, and yet she has that beast inside her – I'm so desperate for a cure to be found, I just thought … well, I don't know what I thought. But when this vampire thing came up, I could see the connection and I knew I had no choice. Forgive me, please. And I promise you, there is nothing else that you don't know of here."

Mike knew instinctively that Roman was speaking the truth and he understood – he had experienced much the same feeling with his own daughter, Adain's, 'differences'. His forgiveness was immediate and absolute, and if anything he felt even more committed to the Strazca than ever before.

Further conversation was brought to an abrupt halt as Beckett burst through the front door, Darius once again in his arms.

Mike and Roman were on the scene immediately.

"What do you need?" Roman asked.

"I need to keep him asleep until we can get organised to help him properly. All our resources at the Sanctuary are gone. There is no anti-HVV serum and not enough donated blood. And I need to keep him … secure."

Roman understood immediately and headed towards the stairs down to the basement. Beckett and Mike followed right behind.

The routine scanning to gain access and entry through the fake bookcase seemed to take forever, but then they were once again in the underground facility. The white-coated Kurt Bauer looked up from a microscope and hurried towards them. One glance at Darius and then at Roman, who nodded almost imperceptibly, was enough. He turned and opened the door to the room adjacent to the sleeping Lowell.

Beckett laid Darius onto the bed and turned to Kurt. "Put him to sleep – I mean *deep* sleep, but I need to be able to wake him quickly. Can you do that?" He nodded towards Lowell's window.

Kurt understood and left the room, returning almost immediately with a tray of glass vials and loaded syringes, one of which he inserted into Darius's vein.

The sharp pain of the needle being inserted into the back of his hand woke him before the drug could be administered; he immediately responded with rage. His face contorted and his vampire strength returned from out of nowhere. The tray of syringes was sent flying against the wall, swiftly followed by Kurt. Darius was in a feeding frenzy and about to get his next meal from Kurt's throat.

Beckett hurled himself across the room and ripped Darius away from Kurt before he could do any damage. His fist connected with Darius's jaw with a sharp crack, his head went back and his body ended up against the opposite wall.

Mike had never seen Beckett in vampire mode and was momentarily shocked, but his friend's demeanour returned to his normal calm as he picked the unconscious Darius up and returned him to the bed.

Moments later the needle was once again in Darius's vein and Kurt drove the drug home, sending him into oblivion.

"I thought he could go into a deep sleep to heal himself … what did you call it … the Long Sleep?" Mike asked.

Beckett shook his head. "It takes a great deal of time and patience to master it – years – and he's responding to the most basic of needs – he's ravenously hungry." He looked at Kurt. "I'm sorry, I should have been prepared. Are you all right?"

Kurt nodded his response. "I will keep him asleep, don't worry. And I have the drug standing by that will counter the effects almost instantly. You just have to say the word?"

Beckett nodded. "I'll be back as soon as I can with a donor. He has fed from me, but he should have human blood now. Too much vampire blood will only increase the hunger. Raven needs rest too. I need you to watch him until I get back, Mike. Lane has gone to meet with her lawyer to arrange for funds to be released immediately. We need to begin rebuilding the Sanctuary without delay. Too many depend upon it to do nothing. She had a call from Mihai – the head of the Council – Vasile Tepes is close to finding something that will aid him in destroying all of the Created. I don't know any more than that, but I believe that Lane does. I don't want to leave Darius, but I need to find a donor for him. As I said, I daren't give him any more vampire blood."

Mike was taking off his jacket. "Take what you need," he said.

CHAPTER TWENTY-NINE: TO TRANSYLVANIA

One phone call from Mihai was all it took for a plane to be waiting for them at Louis Armstrong Airport, outside the city – fuelled and ready to fly them to Bucharest.

As usual, the vampire network was in place and running smoothly and with little delay they were boarding the private Boeing 737 that would take them to Bucharest via London.

Lafayette raised an eyebrow as he boarded the plane that had been stripped inside and now resembled a high-end apartment. The smile from the beautiful cabin attendant revealed her neat fangs, which made him relax. No need for pretence, obviously.

She greeted Mihai with deference. "Patriarch, it is our pleasure to be of service. My name is Rose and I will be here to attend to you and your guest during the ten hour flight to London Heathrow." She returned her smile to Lafayette.

He grinned back at her, imagining the relaxing flight, with plenty of rum, cigars, and possibly a large drink of fresh blood.

Mihai read him. "Forget it, Lafayette. You may have one drink – for the remainder of the flight you will put yourself into the vampire Small Sleep and recoup your energies for what lies ahead. We will be joined in London by Lane Dearing, who will accompany us to Bucharest."

Lafayette's curiosity outweighed his disappointment. "Lane Dearing? She's a high-flyer on the council, is she not?"

Mihai nodded to him as they sat on facing plush sofas and fastened their seat-belts. As per instructions, the plane had begun to taxi to the runway with priority clearance as soon as they had boarded the plane.

"Yes," he replied. "She will be my successor, though she doesn't know it yet."

Lafayette grinned. "Ha! A Matriarch, then. That's new – and very brave of you. Female *and* a Created. The Born are going to love her!"

Mihai's look was enough to quell any further conversation as the plane took off, and once the seat-belt light pinged to allow them more freedom, he walked towards the rear of the plane, where several cubicles housed extremely comfortable beds.

"Sleep, Lafayette – if you know what's good for you."

Mihai's voice was steady and his gaze even steadier, and Lafayette realised then just how much trouble he was about to be in. He claimed a bed and lay down, sleep nowhere near him, his thoughts in free-fall and his longing for his home in the Quarter a powerful stimulant. But Mihai's warning had been clear, and yet here he was, flying towards what now appeared to be more than a spat between the ancients – something he had always avoided at all costs. He forced his heart-rate to slow, his breathing to become almost imperceptible, and his mind clear of all distraction. Slowly, very slowly, the Small Sleep overtook him and he became oblivious to his surroundings and the passing of time. He drew strength into every cell of his body, pulling the energy from his hidden reserves, making him hungry.

Mihai's sleep was troubled. He was reaching out to his maker, the First One – searching the ether for the energy signature of Jean-Baptiste, and finding nothing. He frowned in his sleep.

*

Lane looked tired, but wouldn't admit to it. Her priority on returning home had been Darius and she had neglected to feed. Two of her longest-serving donors met with her and she left with enough blood for herself and for Darius. Now she was returning to Linwood House with a message from Mihai – the future of the Created and the Council lay in the balance, for if Vasile Tepes got his hands on the Bloody Chalice and succeeded in resurrecting Vlad, all bets were off.

Mihai had been clear – they were all needed in what was to come – and what was to come was in Transylvania.

He was en-route from New Orleans having failed to find his maker but had in his company an eighteenth century vampire called Lafayette, who had been a close companion of Jean-Baptiste Vincent, the First One. They would stop off in London to refuel, and pick up Lane and Beckett at the same time. And time, it would seem, was of the essence. She made a quick calculation and decided that given the time Mihai and Lafayette had left New Orleans and the usual flight time to London, she had enough time to get back to Linwood House and collect Beckett. She was adamant that Darius should remain, even though she knew that once he was awake she would have a battle on her hands closer to home.

The miles were eaten up while she tried to relax and focus her vampire senses, and when she walked through the door of the Strazca headquarters she was sharp and alive and ready for the task ahead. Mihai had been convinced that he knew the location of the chalice – inside the fountain in Tirgoviste. It appeared to make sense. Vlad and all of the House of Tepes would have expected it to be removed as far away as possible, never dreaming that it remained within their grasp all the time. Lane smiled at the thought of how angry Vasile would be when he discovered that. The smile faded quickly though – it all depended on who would get to it first.

She hurried down to the underground facility with Roman, anxious to feed Darius with human blood and assuage his hunger long enough to enable more donors to be found.

Beckett stood and pulled her to him; his sense of loss had grown in her absence. She kissed him gently on the forehead.

"Hello, Handsome. Missed me?"

He grinned at her and dragged his fingers through his hair in his characteristic mannerism when he was anxious. "You have no idea, Legs," he said, using his affectionate name for her.

"Well, save it for later, we need to wake Darius. He needs to feed and then go back to sleep. We have a journey ahead."

She sat on the sofa and pulled him down next to her and explained Mihai's message to him. He continued to cast anxious looks at the sleeping Darius; there was no way he wanted to leave him and there was no way that he would abandon Lane either. Still, if Darius was compliant after feeding they would perhaps be able to drug him back into the arms of deep sleep.

He signalled to Kurt, who came immediately.

"Wake him up, please, Kurt. We have to allow him to feed. But be prepared to send him straight back to sleep once he's fed. OK?"

Kurt nodded his understanding and crossed to the bed, syringe in hand.

In moments Darius's eyes fluttered open and Mike was conscious of holding his breath, alert and ready for trouble that didn't materialise. Beckett was at his side in an instant and Lane moved closer to the foot of the bed. It could have been any family scene in any ICU, but this was a newly-turned vampire who had already killed with savagery and the 'parents' were two powerful vampires who held the future of a whole lot of people in their hands.

Mike thought, 'Everything revolves around the next few minutes and I don't know why.'

Darius closed his eyes again and turned his head away, unable to look Beckett in the eye as memories of his previous actions settled squarely in his mind. "I'm so sorry," he said, in a thick voice that disguised nothing of his emotions.

Beckett held his hand. "You gave us all a scare for a minute, but it's OK. Things will settle. You were turned by a vicious and cruel vampire, which means you have his blood rushing through your veins. It also means that his cruelty is also affecting you. It will settle – I promise." His unspoken thoughts were, *'But there will always be that ability within you to be a ruthless killer. Pray God you will learn how to control it.'*

Lane moved around the bed holding a plain pewter goblet. Mike flinched at the contents but refused to look away.

"Here," she said. "You need to feed. *This* way." Her meaning was clear and Darius took the goblet from her and put it to his lips, casting a brief look at Beckett, who smiled and nodded his support. Darius drank long and deep and this time Mike glanced away, feeling that somehow he was witnessing a private moment – a sacrament.

The atmosphere shifted and Beckett visibly relaxed as if a moment of danger had passed. There was almost a feeling of relief palpable in the air – that lasted all of twenty seconds. His expression changed and he moved closer to Darius.

"Son, we have to leave you for a while. I really don't want to have to do this and you know I would NEVER leave you at such a crucial time, but I have no choice – *we* have no choice. I'm leaving you in excellent care and I'll be back before you know it."

It was one of those breath-taking moments that remain deeply etched in a memory forever. Darius's movements were so fast it seemed to Mike that he vanished from the bed and rematerialized at the door.

"I know what this is about and if you imagine for one second that I'm going to lie here while you face this, you're out of your mind. And if you think you can keep me here under chemical cosh, you need to think again. I don't know where this strength is coming from but it's going to take a bigger syringe. Now, can I have some clothes please?"

Mike could do nothing to prevent the laugh that came unbidden – this was the young man he'd begun to get to know. Lane protested but Beckett just went in search of his black leather jacket and pants that had become his favourite, hoping the blood had been cleaned off from Darius's recent savage attacks. Mike followed him.

When Mike caught up with Beckett he stood in front of him, blocking his path back to Darius's room.

"I know that technically this isn't my fight, but I *am* coming with you. Beth is safe here and there is no change in her, nor has there been – and according to you, it is unlikely that there will be anytime soon. So you need to start filling me in, because like it or not, I'm with you in this. Refresh my memory – exactly how *do* you destroy a vampire?"

Beckett's eyes cleared and he relaxed just a fraction. He put his hand on Mike's arm as he laughed involuntarily. "You kill me, Mike."

"Let's bloody well hope not!"

*

Half an hour from London, Rose woke Mihai and Lafayette with ornate goblets of blood. She smiled at Lafayette. "Sorry, no rum for you – Patriarch's orders." She winked at him. "But there is plenty for the return journey. And cigars."

For the first time, he began to wonder if there would *be* a return journey.

The plane landed and taxied to a holding area for refuelling, during which time, a sleek black car pulled up on the tarmac beside them. Lane looked tired, but there

162

were deep lines around her eyes and mouth that deterred Lafayette from introducing himself. Lane nodded to him briefly and greeted Mihai with a kiss on the cheek. Mike smiled at the human gesture.

She cast a glance at Lafayette and Mihai smiled and nodded. "Darius is OK. I will stake my life on it."

Mihai frowned, "You may have to. And Beckett, good to see you again, my friend." He held out his hand to Mike and looked searchingly at Lane.

"This is Mike Travis, he's a special friend of Beckett's and yes, he's human, but he has … experience … in fighting monsters – for want of a better word. It's OK. He's coming with us. Beckett has told him everything that he needs to know on the way."

Mihai frowned.

Lane ignored it and continued. "How sure are you that Vlad is really not dead? And Vasile knows the whereabouts of the Bloody Chalice? How could this happen, Mihai? How?"

"I'm afraid it is true. As for the how …" he shrugged, "it doesn't matter. What is important is that we find it before Vasile Tepes. He is close to getting his hands on the chalice. I told you the seal is not where I left it, but I believe I know where it is now. On Snagov Island in the grave of a monk. But, God willing, it will only serve to distract him. I believe the Chalice is in Tirgoviste – where it always was – but now it is buried beneath the fountain in the town square. Vasile is ahead of us, heading for Snagov. We may yet beat him to it."

She frowned. "And if we don't?"

Mihai's expression didn't change. "Then we have a very big problem."

The plane was refuelled and they were soon taxiing towards the end of the runway, again with priority clearance for take-off. Mihai was busy making calls to the network in Transylvania and once he was satisfied that they would be met at Bucharest airport with transport to

Tirgoviste he once again returned to his bed to gather strength for whatever was coming. Just before the Small Sleep overtook him, he sent a text message to the Council.

Youth and anxiety kept Lafayette from sleep, and Lane took the opportunity to get to know him. After all, they would have to have each other's backs in the not too distant future.

Beckett tried to get Darius to sleep but it was never going to happen.

Four hours later they were stepping onto the tarmac in Bucharest and being ushered into a waiting four-by-four vehicle for the last leg of the journey to Tirgoviste.

CHAPTER THIRTY: BETRAYAL

Lucy clung on to the side of the small boat as Vasile steered it towards the shore of tiny Snagov Island. The grey water of the lake appeared forbidding, as if it knew the reason for Vasile's visit but didn't dare to impede him.

He beached the boat and they strode together towards the old chapel; Lucy keeping pace with him, stride for stride. The gathering dusk sent grey shadows flitting around the interior of the chapel and towards the altar, a grave in the floor caught his attention. He fell to his knees to examine the inscription on the lid.

"This is the grave of the monk. Move back," he said gruffly to Lucy. His vampire strength enabled him to lift the granite top with ease and he pushed it away as if it had been fashioned from air.

The skeletal remains of the monk grinned up at him and he made an impatient grab at the bony fingers that, in death, clutched the other half of Lucy's pendant. The dragon appeared to be smiling and Vasile took it as an omen. Several sharp cracks announced the finger bones breaking as he wrenched the pendant free with a cry of triumph. Without warning he snatched its other half roughly from around Lucy's neck.

Putting the two halves together, he peered at the back through the falling gloom. He was angry: could it be that simple? All the years that he had searched for the chalice, had it really never moved from its original home?

His senses were on full alert and he spun around as the assailant prepared to strike. His arm flew up to deflect the blow and he threw himself towards the vampire that was bearing down on him again. He recognised him as one of his cousins – he was betrayed. He allowed himself a glance at Lucy, but the shout of warning died on his lips as he saw her vulpine smile of satisfaction.

It was only a split-second but it was enough – his assailant brought the massive stake down hard into his chest and shoved him backwards into the monk's tomb, where he landed on top of the skeletal remains, blood bubbling around his mouth. His eyes were fixed on Lucy, asking the question – why?

She knelt at the side of the tomb and snatched both halves of the pendant from his weakening grasp and smiled at him.

"Why? You of all of us should know the answer to that. Because: why would I settle for you, when I can be the one to resurrect Vlad and be his consort, when he will once again be head of the most powerful vampire House? Once Vlad is back, you will be nothing again." She glanced at the pendant in her hands. "Thank you for retrieving it for me, I'll be going now. Die quietly Vasile, this is a holy place."

The blood stopped bubbling around his lips and his eyes closed. She waited for several minutes, watching him carefully, reaching out with her vampire senses, and, finally satisfied, she stood up and cast a last glance into the tomb.

"There's a good boy," she said, then allowed herself a harsh laugh. The assailant nodded to her and followed her from the chapel towards the boat. Only when they were safely on the shore did she acknowledge him.

"You did well, Dumitri, you can be sure that Vlad will reward you. Be good enough to drive me to where this leads. I will need some time with it. Perhaps, while you are waiting you could find me some food. I'm hungry."

She let her tongue travel across the pointed canine teeth, ensuring the Dumitri Tepes knew exactly what she meant by 'food'. He nodded to her and guided her back to Vasile's car, speaking into his phone as he walked.

"I have a room for you at the Snagov Club Hotel. There will be a plentiful supply of nourishment there –

providing you don't stay too long."

His meaning was clear – leave before the alarm is raised. She smiled, anticipation heightening her hunger; and if there was one thing she had taken from Vasile it was the lust for the kill. The back of the pendant puzzled her, but she was determined to work it out – the less people that saw it the better. Betrayal was easy and almost a way of life in the House of Tepes.

The room looked out onto the lake and it didn't take long for Dumitri to knock discreetly at the door with a young man slumped against him. Once inside, Dumitri allowed him to fall to the floor and looked away as Lucy fell on him, a feeding frenzy about to be satisfied. He began to wonder if he had chosen wisely. She was, after all, very young in vampire terms, and young vampires were unpredictable. But she had been very persuasive and the thought of being of service to Vlad had convinced him.

When she had drained the body of its life-blood she rose, her lower face covered in gore, and she staggered a little, intoxicated by the feasting. His blood was rich and she felt the power surge through her.

Dumitri was glad to see that there was no blood on the carpet – she hadn't wasted a drop – and he left in search of a laundry cart. When he returned, pushing his prize, he found Lucy sitting on the bed staring at the pendant. He didn't speak, he simply lifted the corpse into the cart and left.

Lucy concentrated hard on the image engraved on the reverse of her pendant in its fullness. It settled in her mind as the image of an ancient fountain. Now she scoured the ether in an effort to place it.

Tirgoviste – the legend of the bloody chalice being placed on the town fountain with the dire warning that to remove it meant death. Vasile had told her of the legend, now she knew it was true. And she knew the hiding place of the chalice.

In the darkness of the tomb inside the chapel on

Snagov Island, Vasile Tepes opened his eyes.

CHAPTER THIRTY-ONE: TOO LATE

The vampire network was working on top form and the car was waiting on the tarmac as their plane taxied to a halt. Mihai was first down the steps and into the car, giving instructions to take them as swiftly as possible to Tirgoviste and checking that the equipment he had requested was present and correct. He knew they would have to wait for darkness to cloak their activities – after all, they could hardly break open the foundations of an ancient fountain in broad daylight and get away with it. He prayed that Vasile Tepes would have the same reservations.

The journey to Tirgoviste took just under 2 hours and for the most part they passed it with small talk. Darius was especially quiet as he took in the countryside of his ancestors. It brought back poisonous memories of his brother Andrei, and how he had killed their parents in a savage attack as a newly-turned, vicious vampire. He remembered how he had vowed to kill him in revenge for those deaths and how in the end it had been Beckett who had done the deed. He swallowed the bitterness that was welling up in his throat and leaned back in the seat with closed eyes. He had seen all he wanted to.

Lafayette, although from the eighteenth century, had never left New Orleans once he had arrived there from Santa Domingo and he was hungry for the experience. It also served to ward off any misgivings about betraying the First One, or what they may be about to face.

Lane and Beckett hardly spoke; deep in preparation for the coming fight that they were sure was to come and knowing it was going to be bloody. Mihai too had his eyes closed but only because he was scanning the ether for signs of Jean-Baptiste but coming up empty. The First

One had always been able to cloak himself and it seemed as though that was the case.

Light was fading as they approached Tirgoviste and Mihai gave instructions to the driver to drop them just outside the centre of the city, to wait for them and to come for them at speed if they called. A single nod of understanding was all the response that was required.

They split into two groups, not wishing to stand out as they made their way to the fountain. Mihai was striding ahead and as Lane and Beckett rounded the corner behind him they were stunned at the sight ahead of them.

The fountain was surrounded by police and the base lay broken open and scattered on the ground.

They were too late.

*

Lucy clutched the bag containing the Bloody Chalice to her as she stepped inside Vasile's home opposite Poenari. Nicolae had returned – where else would he go? And there was nothing to connect him to Davina's escape, even if Vasile knew that she was still alive. This was his home too, where he had lived and served Vasile for many years.

"Miss Lucy – you are alone. Where is my master?"

"He will be here presently," she replied. "He can only be a short while behind me. He sent me home ahead of him to prepare for a special dinner tonight. He bade me tell you to prepare his favourite." She laughed, "I hope you know what that is, because he didn't share it with me. He wanted it to be a surprise, I think."

Nicolae nodded to her. "I do indeed, miss. I will begin the preparations immediately. Is there anything that I can get for you in the meanwhile?"

Lucy shook her head. "No, thank you. I believe I will rest before I get ready, I believe Vasile wants this to be a special evening." She tossed her luxuriant hair and laughed again, as she began to climb the stairs. Once on the landing, she was satisfied that Nicolae had taken himself off to the kitchen and she slipped back down the stairs and down the second staircase to the basement.

Vasile kept the crypt locked and the key on him at all times, but she had taken it from his pocket as he lay in the tomb on Snagov. Her hand shook as she unlocked the door and closed it quietly behind her. She turned a switch which lit the gas torches in their sconces on the wall, creating the atmosphere that Vlad would have been familiar with.

The stone coffin stood in the centre of the room on an ornately carved plinth and she felt a moment's hesitation and anxiety as she approached it. He laid there, not much more than a skeleton with a fine covering of skin and grizzled hair, appearing as one long dead – but she knew how far away from the truth that was.

Suddenly emboldened, she stepped towards the coffin and held out the Bloody Chalice.

"I have what you need Vlad. I have brought it to you and offer myself to you, to stand beside you."

A blinding pain in her head made her gasp as she heard the 'voice' from the desiccated remains inside her head.

"You have done well, and you shall have your reward. Come closer."

She hesitated, suddenly overcome with anxiety, but this was no time to back away, she had come this far and her future as consort to the most feared vampire was assured. All she had to do was to open a vein and allow her blood to pool in the chalice and put it to Vlad's lips. A surge of energy washed through her and she raised her wrist to her lips, feeling her canine fangs sharp against her lower lip as she ripped open her wrist and allowed her blood to pour into the bottom of the chalice.

A hiss came from the dried lips in the coffin and she felt the thrill of triumph as her blood mingled with the centuries-old stain within the chalice itself. She didn't know what she had expected – some miraculous alchemy producing a red, foaming, magical elixir? What actually happened was nothing. The hiss from inside the coffin carried with it an insistence, an urgency that brought a response from somewhere deep within her chest. She leaned over the coffin, half-expecting Vlad's eyes to be open, but not a muscle had moved. And yet she could 'hear' him, urging her to put the chalice to his long-dead mouth. She imagined that she could see his eyes, imploring her to get on with it.

She lowered the chalice into the coffin, positioning it over the dried-out lips, tilting it ever so slightly, watching the blood edging closer to the lip of the chalice, close enough to allow the first drop to fall – apparently in slow-motion – onto the mouth of Vlad Dracula. She allowed herself a nervous laugh – she had seen the movies, especially the old ones, where the blood dripped onto Christopher Lee's mouth and his eyes snapped open and …

The hand that hit her hard on the side of her face reached out and grabbed the chalice before it fell to the ground and spilled its content onto the stone floor. Such a waste was not to be tolerated.

He raised the chalice to his lips and drank deeply from it, then turned his attention to the unconscious Lucy. Another waste. Such a shame.

He bent low over her inert body and opened her throat in one smooth movement, gorging himself on her blood before even a drop fell to the floor. He felt his energy returning, his strength beginning to surge through him again. He closed his eyes to enjoy the pleasure of the sensations, sighing in satisfaction.

He pushed Lucy's dead body aside with a contemptuous kick, betrayal still bitter in Vasile Tepes' throat.

"Now, old man, you will feed on Tepes blood and the ritual to restore you will be as written."

He closed his eyed in order to appreciate the moment.

172

A bony hand reached up from the stone coffin and grasped his wrist. "Not here! You know where."

Images of the ruins at Poenari flooded his mind and his eyes snapped open. Vlad had not moved a muscle, but his communication had been imperative.

CHAPTER THIRTY-TWO: THE FIRST ONE

Mihai cursed, long and loud, and shrugged Lane's consoling hand away from his shoulder.

"I need to think! We can't afford to be this far behind him. If he manages to wake Vlad – well, let's just say it won't be good."

Mike was beginning to regret accompanying them, feeling more and more like a spare wheel, not really understanding their conversations but catching up rapidly – he was a fast learner. And what he was learning made him uneasy.

Darius was looking tired and claiming most of Beckett's attention, so Mike was relying on Lafayette for conversation and company. He had warmed to the Louisiana vampire and was fascinated by talk of his human life as a slave on the plantations of Santa Domingo and then New Orleans before his life was forever changed when he crossed paths with a thirsty vampire.

Lafayette's tone was light-hearted, "You haven't asked me what most people do – those that don't know I'm a vampire, that is."

"And that would be?" Mike replied.

"Voodoo! Is it real? Is it practiced widely in New Orleans?"

Mike laughed. He was no stranger to the Dark Arts and the shadow world of demons. "I've had the odd brush or two with the occult world and its inhabitants, so I'm guessing Voodoo is just as prolific as the European Black Magic. I can't say I'm familiar with its structure or rituals though. Maybe I should visit when this is over. You up to playing host to a demon hunter, Lafayette? Or would that ruin your street cred?"

Lafayette grinned, flashing his white teeth. "OK, then, I deserved that. So, if I may be so bold, what the hell are you doing here?"

Mike became serious again, "Beckett is a friend – a good friend. He's in trouble, I'm here. He's done the same for me. I'm ready for whatever and I'm not averse to removing heads from deserving candidates, if you follow me. I'm not quite up to speed on vampires in general and this one in particular, but I catch on real quick. I won't get in your way."

Lafayette seemed reassured and gave Mike a friendly pat on the shoulder. Mike nodded his understanding. Lafayette had needed to know that Mike had his back as much as he had his, and that, when the chips were down, he wouldn't be a liability.

Mike wandered over to Beckett. "How's he doing?" he asked, nodding at Darius.

"He's OK. He'd be better in the Sanctuary, but that can't happen, so he's better with us than not. He's come through the worst, but there's a darkness inside him spawned by his creator – another fucking Tepes! It makes him unpredictable."

"Tell me what I can do, whatever it is."

Beckett nodded his appreciation and gave Mike a smile he didn't really feel. "It's not looking good here, Mike. If Vasile has the chalice and performs the Waking Ritual …"

Mike interrupted him. "The Waking Ritual?"

Beckett sighed – the thought of waking Vlad filled him with dread and it seemed as if merely talking about it would bring down calamity. Still, Mike had to know what was coming.

"You know about the Long Sleep, when vampires voluntarily hibernate when weary of centuries of living, or when they are seriously wounded and need lengthy healing, well, sometimes they sleep for too long or are too seriously wounded to bring themselves out of it. It doesn't happen often but, when it does, there is a ritual feeding – you could relate it to a blood transfusion – that will wake them up. There is a legend about this Bloody Chalice among those that believe Vlad was never killed outright; that performing the Waking Ritual with the Bloody Chalice, so steeped in blood that its very fabric is infused with it, will bring Vlad back. If that happens, all of the rebel Houses will align behind him and the Council will be wiped out. Blood-lust will rule our kind and once the Created are gone there will be nothing to control them."

Mike raised an eyebrow. "I knew about the chalice from what you were saying before, but Vlad? Really? You're talking Dracula, right? I mean …"

"Mike you know better than anyone that folk-tales, legends and myths all start with a grain of truth. Vlad the Impaler, AKA Vlad Dracula, was the most powerful vampire to walk this earth, more powerful even than the First One. If the legends are true and his body still lies waiting for the Waking Ritual and the chalice is found – which is pretty much a foregone conclusion now – he will lead the Born into another bloody war which will only end when all the Created are destroyed." He looked around. "Where is Mihai?"

Lane came over to him. "He said he needed to reach out to any of the Council that could hear him, we need as much help as we can get. I believe he is also trying to reach Jean-Baptiste Vincent. He is bitter that he missed him in New Orleans, that his maker is ignoring his pleas for help against everything that he taught him – that the maker has to teach his infant, watch over him as he finds his way in our world, counsel him and come to his assistance when asked – just like a human parent." Her face was paler than usual.

"How are you holding up?" Beckett asked her quietly.

"Don't worry, I'll be OK. I'm up to it, if that's what you mean. I know I look like shit, and not yet back to full capacity, but I won't let you down, Handsome."

Despite their situation, Beckett smiled at her; a warm smile that said everything. "You never look like shit, Legs. Not to me."

There was a tense moment when nothing else mattered to Beckett except her feelings. Had they changed since the Long Sleep? Before that everything had seemed possible between them, now ….

The moment seemed to last a life-time – a vampire life-time – as she read him, and then without another word she pulled him to her and kissed him full on the mouth. "Does that answer your question?"

He grinned. "I guess so."

"Good, make it last until this crap is over."

He sobered at the thought of the upcoming battle for their lives and the lives of all the Created. It would all hang on what took place in the coming hours – a short, intense fight with Vasile and his followers, or, if they lost, a long and bloody war amongst the entire vampire world. But then the knowledge of her feelings for him buoyed him up and he was ready to take on Vlad himself.

Mihai moved with vampire-speed, unseen, through the streets of Tirgoviste, until he came to the outskirts and a dark, empty, church. He settled down near the ornate screen and searched the ether, calling out to any vampire loyal to the council to come to their aid. He didn't feel any response. The threat of Vlad returning, it seemed, was enough to test the loyalty of the staunchest council supporter. He turned his focus onto his maker.

"Jean-Baptiste! I know you hear me! I sense your presence, make yourself known to me! I implore you. You MUST know what is at stake. How can you ignore me? How can you be so selfish as to take yourself into the Eternal Sleep, because I know that is what you are contemplating? Selfish and irresponsible! Yes – irresponsible because as the First One, we are ALL your responsibility. Damn you to hell! Answer me! I KNOW you hear me!"

The silence deafened him.

"Then fuck you! Know this, my maker, if we come through this I will hunt you down and help you into the Eternal Sleep myself! *You bastard!*"

There was a sudden movement of air behind him and Jean-Baptiste Vincent stepped from behind a heavily carved pillar.

"Such hot words, Mihai. I thought you would have more faith in me. "

Mihai spun around, his countenance livid with unspent fury.

"*Why? Why did you not answer me?* You knew I was there, in New Orleans, why run out on me? On all of us? Have you become a coward as well?"

"Because, Mihai, I believed that after millennia, you were amply capable of looking after yourself. Was I mistaken?"

Mihai shook his head with sadness. How could his maker have become so cold, so callous? "You know it's not about me."

The First One lowered his head. "No," he said quietly, "no, it isn't. There seems to have grown a lack of trust between us, Patriarch. I was wrong. But you are right; I have many times contemplated the Eternal Sleep – selfish, yes – irresponsible, maybe – but never a coward. I left New Orleans to get ahead of the game, but I was too late also. Vasile Tepes does indeed have the Bloody Chalice and will perform the Waking Ritual on Vlad – and yes, Vlad was one of my biggest mistakes. I turned him in the hope that it would help him bring the people of Transylvania out of the darkness, instead it made him into the bloodiest ruler they had ever seen."

"You cannot allow this," Mihai continued, his rage subsiding but his intensity still on fire. "You cannot allow this to happen. It is your responsibility to stand with us!"

Jean-Baptiste nodded slowly, "I'm here, am I not? I suggest we collect the others and waste no more time on insulting each other."

Together they sped, unseen again, through Tirgoviste, "You know where he is?" Mihai asked.

"I know where he is headed – to Poenari."

Mihai almost spat the words. "His castle ruins."

"Indeed. It seems it is not only Vlad that is to be restored."

"You have the authority to command support. Why haven't you done so?" Mihai demanded.

"Because if we succeed here, there will be no need to put so many lives at risk. And, before you say it, we do not stand a better chance with more numbers. There is to be dark magic abroad here tonight, Mihai. An army won't make any difference. Yes, blood will be spilled, it is inevitable, but fate will also play its part."

They arrived, almost materialising in front of the others; something that Mike would never get used to.

Lane appeared unmoved by Mihai's companion, and Lafayette nodded at his former employer. "Sir," he said.

Beckett and Darius instinctively took a step back and Mike closed in on them. "Mihai?" Beckett challenged, "Who is your friend?"

Lane read his resentment and stepped forward, "Allow me to introduce Jean-Baptiste Vincent, the First One. And yes, I literally mean, the First One. We are all 'descended', if that is the word, from him."

They took in the tall, dark olive-skinned man who stood before them, dressed as he always was in Louisiana colonial gentleman style, in a cream linen suit, white shirt, and white bow tie. He looked ridiculous.

He read them collectively, as only the First One could. "Yes, I'm afraid I didn't have time to change. But I expect before the night is out, I shall have need to and will find some suitable clothing as we travel. Shall we go?"

"Where?" demanded Beckett, unmoved by the presence of the first of all vampires, the most ancient of their kind. He was simply pissed off by Mihai's high-handedness and more than ready for a fight.

Lane was increasingly alarmed at Beckett's resentment of Mihai and answered before the Patriarch could. "I'm guessing we are headed deep into the Carpathians. Vasile's stronghold is there, but so too is the ruin of Vlad's castle on the crags above the Arges River, at Poenari. Am I right?"

Mihai smiled at her and nodded. Beckett scowled. Mike was simply happy that something positive was happening at last.

Out of Mike's hearing she pressed Mihai. "What do we have in the way of weapons?"

"Our personal ones, and there are a few blades. The guns and silver nitrate-coated bullets didn't make it. Our network is good, but not that good that we can get guns and ammunition onto a plane, even if it is *our* plane. The blades were already concealed on board as standard but that's it. We haven't had time to gather more since we were here."

The journey to Poenari by road was usually around two hours, but at that time of year, with snow already falling, the main highway was going to be almost impossible, possibly closed. Although 'closed' didn't mean much to vampires. Still, Mihai had foreseen such events and their vehicle was a Peugot Traveller, eight-seater and an all-terrain monster that may have lacked a little in speed, but would get them to their destination, road closed or not.

Snow was settling now in Tirgoviste, so the further into the Carpathians they ventured, the more certain it was to be a white-out. Mike's apprehension returned and his thoughts went to Beth, in her own world, safe in the care of Roman at the Strazca headquarters. He sent her a silent message, or it may have been a prayer.

CHAPTER THIRTY-THREE: TO POENARI

The Vampire Rite of Waking, more commonly referred to as The Waking Ritual, is magic at its blackest, and, if not performed absolutely correctly, with no mistakes or errors of judgement, is likely to cost the life of the one performing the ritual along with the one they were aiming to 'wake'.

In his present state, Vlad, who had been 'asleep' for six centuries, after receiving what would have been mortal wounds in a human, lay on the borderland between life and death. It was only his consciousness that kept him from slipping into the Eternal Sleep, where no vampire, not even Vlad, could return from; it would be vampire death.

Vasile was calm as he prepared for the ritual. He called Nicolae.

"Sir?" Nicolae kept his head down, it was always best that way when Vasile was in one of his moods. And he especially didn't want his master reading his thoughts and discovering his treachery over Davina.

"How long have you served this House, Nicolae?"

"Most of my life, sir. I came here as a boy, as you know."

"You know, don't you, the history of my House?"

Head stayed down, "Yes, sir, and I know the honour that serving you has brought me."

Vasile nodded and appeared to be thinking; in fact he was trying to read Nicolae. Had it not been for Alexis Vasilakis putting protection on him, Nicolae would have been an open book to Vasile. The fact that he couldn't troubled him, but he let it go; after all, Nicolae would be serving him for the last time soon enough.

He appeared to come to a decision and strode towards the stairs to the crypt.

"I have business at my great-grandfather's castle and I need you to assist me." He refrained from adding '*one last time*'.

Nicolae nodded his understanding; suddenly he regretted his mortality.

"We are crossing the Arges River, Nicolae, returning to my ancestral home to perform an important ceremony. It will be rebuilt once again into our sanctuary. Have no doubt on that."

Nicolae didn't.

"You have always been forbidden to enter the locked room beneath us, but you will follow me now."

Nicolae kept several paces behind Vasile as he descended the stairs to the crypt. It was true, he had never been inside the locked room, but he wasn't stupid, and he had worked out years ago what, or who, was down there. Now he was certain of it. The fact that Vasile was about to share this with him, now after all his years of loyal service, told a grim story – his life expectancy was about to be radically reduced.

His thoughts went to Davina, relieved that she was safe with Alexis Vasilakis, at least he would die knowing he had protected her, that she was safe. He had a choice – he could go with Vasile and do his best to do as much damage as he could before his life was claimed in some damnable rite, or he could cut and run. The second option, at his time of life didn't involve much in the way of running, and he knew that Vasile would be on him in a heart-beat ready to rip out his throat. Either way, his future was short-term. He decided to go along and try and wreak as much havoc as he could before the end.

He followed Vasile several more paces behind than usual, his eyes still cast down, as the present Head of the House of Tepes opened the heavy door leading to the crypt.

"Have you never been tempted to come down here, Nicolae? Curious about what lies behind this door?"

Nicolae shook his head, "No, sir. You forbade it."

Vasile smiled a satisfied smile. "You have always been loyal, Nicolae." The thought did not, however, make him reconsider Nicolae as a fitting candidate to bleed out to fill Vlad's veins in a feeding frenzy once the ritual was complete and Vlad had drunk Tepes blood from the chalice, restoring him as Vlad Dracula, Head of the House of Tepes. "Your loyalty will be rewarded and you shall witness a miracle. At Poenari I will perform a ceremony that will once again make the House of Tepes feared throughout Transylvania and beyond."

He stepped aside and ushered Nicolae into the crypt, allowing the door to close behind him.

"Come," Vasile said, "I will introduce you to your new master."

He strode over to the stone coffin and looked down onto the desiccated features of the man who had been the most feared and merciless ruler, Vlad Dracula, Prince of Wallachia, now Transylvania.

Nicolae followed his gaze. Could this pitiful cadaver really be him? Could he really be brought back? No blood flowed in the veins, no heart beat beneath the brittle ribcage, and no breath filled the dried up lungs. How was this possible?

Suddenly, Nicolae felt overcome; his breath caught in his chest and an icy hand clutched at his heart, sending shock-waves throughout his body making him feel faint. There was ringing in his ears and a trickle of cold sweat ran down his back. He could feel his bladder slacken – it didn't take much at his age. And then he was looking into the open, desolate eyes of the most cruel of the vampire race and he knew – he knew that the seemingly impossible was about to become a reality – Vlad Dracula was going to rise.

He closed his eyes and opened them again slowly.

Vlad's eyes were closed as before and he knew instinctively that they had never opened, just as he knew that life remained in the skeletal form lying on the frigid stone on a blanket of frozen snow.

And he prayed.

CHAPTER THIRTY-FOUR: ANOTHER MARINESCU

Mihai dismissed the driver of their vehicle – there was no point in sending an innocent member of their network to a certain death, and a bloody one at that. Some of those in the employ of the Council knew that they worked for vampires and had been entrusted with their codes of conduct and their secrets. Most of them had been victims, one way or another, of those vampires who flouted the code and fed without regard for human life.

Radu Lupescu was such a man.

He still woke at night screaming his mother's name, bathed in sweat and sick to his stomach. He still recalled vividly the images and memories of the night she was dragged from her bed and her throat ripped out as the vampire Andrei Marinescu gorged on her blood and left her drained of all her life-giving fluid in a mangled heap on the bedroom floor, where he was in hiding under the bed. He had been four years old at the time.

He had been taken in and raised by a man who, he subsequently discovered, was a vampire – a vampire that lived on the right side of the tracks; a vampire with a conscience and a responsibility to the victims of the ruthless, and who brought him up to understand that, just like humans, not all vampires were evil. Radu's conviction had never been broken and when his adoptive father was slain by one of the Tepes family, he went straight to the Council and offered himself in service.

But he never forgot the face of Andrei Marinescu; it would haunt him forever. And now, he was looking at that face all over again.

Darius had grown to resemble his vicious brother,

Andrei, in physical likeness only, and it had been his life-long mission to avenge his own family whom Andrei had slain without a second thought. It was while Darius was hunting Andrei, that he had come into contact with Beckett and Lane.

Darius was exceedingly pale and Beckett realised that the turning had left him in a more weakened and ravenously hungry state than he had anticipated. It scared him, because in that state Darius was unpredictable. In addition to that, he had taken into himself the blood of another callous and ruthless vampire, feeding on the very DNA of pure evil. It was going to take some time for it to be diluted and eradicated, and that had to done in a controlled environment. Not here in the wilds of the Carpathian Mountains, where the very air they breathed was tainted by the name Tepes.

Radu was in conflict.

He had sworn his loyalty to the Council and had been proud to serve them in their network in several capacities, and he had always volunteered to drive Mihai whenever he was in Romania. But here, right in front of him, there could be no mistake in the Marinescu lineage.

He turned to Mihai. "Thank you, Mihai, but I would prefer to drive you onwards. The roads are treacherous now with the lying snow and there is much more to fall yet this night. I am used to it – you will be safer if I drive you."

Mihai looked up into the snow-laden sky. Already the flakes were falling heavy and fast, settling on their clothes and hair. There was logic in what Radu said, but still, the thought of an innocent death being down to them left a nasty taste in his mouth. He was about to protest when Radu spoke up again.

"I would consider it a breach of trust and negligent of my sworn duty to abandon you to these conditions. Now, if you would please get into the vehicle, we will go. I understand from your conversations that there is a certain degree of haste involved?"

Mihai smiled at him and nodded. "Thank you Radu, we will be honoured for you to drive us to Poenari."

They were mostly quiet on the drive, all aware of the hazardous conditions that Radu was negotiating and all deep in thought about whether they would reach Poenari in time to stop Vasile raising Vlad and unleashing the darkest of evil into the world.

Mihai sat next to Radu, with Mike, Beckett and Darius behind and Lane and Lafayette with Jean-Baptiste in the rear seats. Mike kept his voice low, questions mounting and needing answers.

"I need to know what to expect here, Beckett. I gather it's going to be a blood-bath. But there are seven of us against one; seems like good odds to me. But that's too simple isn't it? So, take your mind off the kid for a minute and tell me."

"I'm sorry, Mike," he glanced at Darius and nodded his understanding that he had neglected Mike's urgent need for knowledge before taking on Vasile, pre-occupied as he had been by Darius in crisis. He began to regret taking him with them, unpredictable as he was right then.

He continued, "Vlad has been in the Long Sleep for too long. He isn't able to wake up on his own and so there is going to be the Waking Ritual. Usually, it's a ritual to Shemsu, the Blood God of the Ancient Egyptians, but that's just window dressing. Basically, it boils down to the equivalent of a blood transfusion only not in a pleasant way. Vlad's veins by now will carry little in the way of blood and need to be filled, in what amounts to feeding him blood – a lot of blood. This time it's different, because of the Bloody Chalice. You know the history of that, and *with* that and the gorging on blood, Vasile intends to restore Vlad."

Mike frowned. "A lot of blood? Forgive my curiosity here, but where exactly is that coming from? I'm beginning to feel like Meals-On-Wheels here."

Beckett was in no mood for Mike's sarcasm. "Vasile isn't expecting us, so I doubt we are the planned source of it. He will already have a sacrifice there – knowing or unknowing – he won't care which. My money is on the old man that lives with him."

"Not some voluptuous female from the local village?"

"Forget the movies, Mike, especially the bad ones; this is no joke!"

"See me laughing? It's just that I would have thought there would be more vitality in blood from a younger source, that's all. Two more questions: why an Ancient Egyptian god, Shemwhatever, when these guys are in Transylvania? And secondly, can we expect any help here?"

Mihai turned around to answer him. "I'll answer your first question, Mike. Ancient Egypt is where it began. It was my home. It is where the First One was created and where the blood-cult worshipping the god Shemsu also began. In the temple at Dendera, Shemsu was worshipped as *Lord of Blood, Slaughterer of the Gods and He Who Dismembers Bodies*. He had the power to raise the dead with sacrificial blood. He was also god of the oil and wine, and was not averse to ripping the head off a wrong-doer and putting it in the wine-press to extract the blood from it."

"Nice," Mike said, under his breath.

"He is still seen as the Blood God of the Vampires by many – especially Vasile and his followers. In answer to your second question – can we expect any help? – I think not. I have been searching the ether, trying to contact other vampires, but the name of Tepes still creates 'obedience' in these parts, so, no, no-one is going to fuck with the House of Tepes. It's us and that's it. Any more questions?"

"Good to know," Mike muttered. "Oh, yes … I do have another question. Do we have any weapons?" The irritation in his voice was blatant.

Lane joined the conversation. "Mostly hand-to-hand,

some of it modern versions of the traditional stake in the heart. Decapitation is the only sure way."

"Again, good to know," he said dryly.

Mike settled back down to brood over why the hell he had become entangled in a vampire war, until the realisation dawned that the rogue vampires were no different to demons – a threat to humanity. Question answered, he tried to switch off in preparation.

Beckett was acutely aware of Darius's anxiety level rising. Suddenly, Darius leaned forwards, "What the hell are you watching me for? Like what you see? You want some of me? That it?"

Mihai spun around. "What the hell, Darius?"

Darius prodded Radu in the back hard. "He keeps watching me in the goddamn mirror, instead of keeping an eye of the fucking road, which is getting deeper and deeper in snow in case no-one noticed! What the fuck is wrong with you?" This last was directed at Radu.

Radu cleared his throat. "I'm sorry, sir. I have been keeping an eye on the road behind us, not you. I'm sorry if you thought otherwise."

Beckett put a restraining hand on Darius' arm. "Sit back and try and relax. It's not far now."

Darius shrugged the hand away, but sat back, his eyes dark and watchful, staring into the driver's rear-view mirror, waiting for the image of Radu's eyes to appear there, watching him.

Radu was shaken. Clearly, Darius was aggressive and carried the Marinescu stamp about him – he needed to be more discreet. He had insisted on accompanying them because, contrary to his loyalty to Mihai and the Council, Darius had awakened in him a burning desire for revenge that he had believed was quenched years previously. He didn't like it, but he knew that, if he got the chance, he would take that revenge and the consequences. He wasn't able to kill Andrei, but the brother would do.

He kept his eyes on the road and was relieved to see

that the snow had eased off a little, although there was a whole night of it to come.

Whatever the outcome at Poenari, they would be lucky to leave there, unless they could make it to the little town of Curtea Des Arges beside the icy river.

Darius was silent and brooding for the remainder of the journey, on edge and hungry beyond words. Beckett was silently communicating his worry to Lane which was being picked up by Mihai and Lafayette, creating tension that was palpable.

As predicted, the road through the Carpathians was closed and massive concrete barriers had been erected to prevent drivers from ignoring the closure. Radu brought the car to a crawling halt in front of the huge and heavy barrier bearing the 'Road Closed' sign.

Mihai was out of the car in a blur and, using his supreme vampire strength, he hurled the huge concrete barrier over the edge of the road and onto the valley floor as if it had been a troublesome pebble. He returned to the car with snow already settled on his coat and long dark hair like a frozen shawl.

"Let's go," he said.

Radu took a deep breath, knowing that they risked the car going into the ravine at the side of the road if he lost his concentration for one minute. He would have to put Darius out of his head until later – later, when he would have the opportunity to take his revenge.

Barely half an hour later they arrived at the foot of the crags above which the ruin of Vlad's castle perched like a watchful eagle.

Mike sighed; he had wasted his time. The climb up the fourteen hundred steps was hard enough, but slick with snow, he would be a liability.

Becket read him.

"You'll be fine, follow us slowly or wait with Radu in the car."

Radu heard the conversation. "If you please, sir, I will

accompany you to the top."

Mihai frowned; they couldn't waste time on stragglers and it was obvious that they were not going to be able to take the steps in huge leaps as they, the vampires, would. He didn't give Mike the opportunity to argue; he simply grabbed hold of him and leaped up the first bunch of steps, taking Mike with him. Lafayette did the same with Radu, Beckett, and Lane following close behind. Jean-Baptiste was ahead of them all.

At the top of the mountain they could see lights flickering in the ruins; Vasile Tepes was obviously already there.

CHAPTER THIRTY-FIVE: THE WAKING RITUAL

One Hour Earlier:

Vasile had charged Nicolae with carrying a large case containing Vlad's Order of the Dragon investiture robes, along with the gold medal bearing the symbols of the Order and the family crest. Nicolae carried them uncomplainingly, despite the weight of the burden that had nothing to do with how heavy the actual items were. With each step, the weight seemed to increase but he didn't slow his pace and climbed the steps as if they were nothing; determination to create as much havoc as possible kept him going. He knew if he was going to stand any chance against Vasile, it would have to be when he was consumed by the ritual, distracted enough to pay no heed to his ageing servant.

Vasile was not dressed in his usual sharp suit, the value of which would have fed a family of four from the Romanian countryside for a week, but he wore his own centuries old clothes, befitting the awakening of Prince Vlad. Around his neck hung a replica of Vlad's medal, but his was in silver – he had no wish to piss off Vlad Dracula right from the start. He had carried his ancestor in his arms from the foot of the crags, taking the thousand and then some steps in great bounds, all the time watching Nicolae to ensure his obedience in following him.

In what remained of Vlad's great hall, a fire burned in the hearth, strange blue flames danced above the burning logs and the smoke layered the air in the absence of a chimney as Vasile began the ceremony.

Nicolae remained at the edge of the proceedings, awaiting instructions or a time when he could act. Torches had been attached to the remaining stones that had once been the wall of this great castle and Nicolae had lit each and every one of them, knowing that they would never be a beacon to the curious in this weather when no-one would be venturing from their own hearth – and knowing, also, that any local seeing lights at the castle ruins would know better than to interfere. He was on his own. He said a prayer in readiness for his end.

Vasile took great care in putting the ancient robes around his ancestor 's skeletal form as he lay on the stone floor before the fire. He signalled to Nicolae to bring the case to him once again. Nicolae bowed his head and obeyed, wary of what might still be inside that had created such an immense burden to carry. Surely not just the robes?

Vasile opened the case with great care and removed a large object that was wrapped in old silk. Nicolae held his breath; a sudden and stark terror engulfed him as he looked at the shape beneath the draping fabric. The thought that his prayer would have gone unheard because God had no place there, passed swiftly and silently through his mind. Vasile removed the old silk and allowed it to fall to the floor.

In his hands he held the Bloody Chalice and a golden ankh – the Ancient Egyptian symbol for life.

Nicolae crossed himself and realised that a foolish old man such as he could do nothing against this force of evil. He was undone and had merely to await his end. Vasile seemed to grow threefold in stature, a trick of the light perhaps; nevertheless he struck an imposing figure standing over Vlad.

He reached down to his belt beneath the outer robe and took a curved dagger from its sheath and lay it beside the chalice. Nicolae held his breath as Vasile appeared to be waiting for something.

Suddenly, the torch flames behaved as if a gust of wind had caught them, but the night air was still and the snow was falling silently around them.

Lights danced in the periphery of the castle walls and, one by one, members of the House of Tepes filed into what remained of the great hall. Constantin Tepes led them, all of the most prominent members of the Tepes clan, and all wearing replicas of the Vlad's medal around their necks – theirs in bronze. Nicolae dropped his head as his last hope of causing chaos died.

He was alone and he would die alone. And bloody.

Vasile acknowledge the gathering of the House and began the ceremony.

He picked up the golden ankh and kissed it, held it against his heart and began to intone the ritual.

"This is the symbol of life, the symbol of the ancient heritage of the House of Tepes. Blood sustains us and makes us strong. Every breath and every sweet drop of blood is a celebration of what we are. Let this ankh be our constant reminder of the life-blood that is so very precious and the darkness that encircles our souls. We are the many-born. We are the Immortal. Eternal we wander the aeons, feeding on the gift of blood that keeps us incarnate, unchanging through the years. We move from lifetime to lifetime, feeding on the blood of the weak to become even stronger. We rejoice in the blood and call upon you, Shemsu, Lord of Blood to restore our ancestor Vlad Dracula, to vital life once more."

He picked up the chalice and the curved dagger and drew the blade across his own wrist, allowing the blood to spill into the chalice. He allowed it to flow until it had half-filled the chalice and the wound on his wrist began to close. He nodded to Constantin who stepped forwards baring his wrist.

Vasile drew the blade across it, allowing more Tepes blood to pour into the chalice, signalling Constantin to stop the blood-flow after only a moment or so. Then, one by one, the remaining Tepes members came forward to add their blood to the chalice.

197

Vasile returned to face Vlad, raised the chalice and plunged the ankh deep inside. The air became still and even the snow appeared to slow its descent. And then, the apparently impossible happened. The blood began to bubble like the early flow of lava and then to increase in viscosity and volume, filling the chalice and overflowing over Vasile's hand.

A look of triumph covered his face and his voice became higher and more insistent, calling repeatedly and frenzied for their Blood God to appear.

CHAPTER THIRTY-SIX: TO THE DEATH

Jean-Baptiste had been ahead of them and he turned back at the sight of the flaming torches of the Tepes clan.

"As I suspected," he told them, Vasile is not alone. The main members of the House of Tepes are with him. We are outnumbered. Considerably." He turned to Mike and Radu. "This is not your fight; if you leave now no-one will think any the worse of you."

Mike's answer was to grab a large, lethal-looking machete from Lane.

Radu's eyes and mind were fixed on Darius. "No. I'll stay," he said.

"Stay close," Beckett said to Darius, whose response was lost in the falling snow.

They tossed aside their bulky coats which would only hamper their movements, Darius kept his black leather jacket against the biting cold. They approached the ruins with caution, trying to keep the crunching of the snow underfoot to a minimum and hoping that Vasile and his crew were too engrossed in the ritual to focus their vampire hearing elsewhere.

Their first sight of Vasile brought everything to an abrupt head.

The over-flowing chalice was down to Vlad's chest which now lay open, the bloody ankh protruding from the gaping wound and Vasile was pouring the Tepes blood directly over the old vampire's heart.

"Blood of life, restore you! Blood of Tepes, restore you! Your Bloody Chalice, restore you!"

Moments frozen in time when it seemed as if no-one moved a muscle, no hearts beat, as they all watched the

199

blood coating the desiccated heart, which appeared to absorb the blood and restore itself. Mike shook his head to clear the image, and that seemed to galvanise the others.

Beckett rushed towards Vasile, blade raised, but the House of Tepes was not so easily vanquished and, as Vlad's heart began to fill with Tepes blood once again, other blood was flowing.

Vasile was enraged at the interruption of the ceremony and flew to meet Beckett head on, curved blade still in hand. As Beckett's rage seethed, he could only see Lane, lying broken in Greece, on the brink of death in his arms, and the Long Sleep of five years as she healed in the old monastery. It was fuelled by the knowledge that this heap of vileness was about to bring back the instrument of death to all the Created. His vision became part of the red spectrum of hatred for Vasile that had been brewing for too long. He lunged at him, catching him across the top of the arm.

It did nothing. Lane appeared behind Vasile, but was pulled away by one of the Tepes clan. Beckett was attacked from behind and the inevitable confrontation had to wait.

Suddenly they were all fighting for their lives and the white snow underfoot was turning red. Each one of them focussed on their own survival and the death of their opponents – each with their own adrenaline pounding through their veins to their own tune.

Mike had rushed towards a large Tepes who was lunging towards him with a dagger pulled from his belt. So, this was to be a knife-fight after all. He could do that.

But he was unprepared for the speed and strength that was launched at him and was momentarily taken off guard. The Tepes raised his blade and was bringing it down swiftly when he suddenly changed his expression of rage to one of surprise, halted, and dropped his blade as his head parted company with his neck and fell onto the blood-slicked snow. Darius stood behind the falling body, blood spattered across his face, a wild look in his eyes.

"Thanks, Kid," Mike muttered before swinging back towards another enraged vampire.

The sound of blade against blade, the heaving bodies, the hissing of wounded vampires on both sides, the smell of blood; all became a sickening cocktail of sensations that threatened to overwhelm.

A sharp cry followed by a blood-freezing gurgle announced the demise of another Tepes as Lane despatched his head in the manner of Darius's strike.

But still they kept coming. It was a matter of math, really. They were still fighting uneven odds.

In the periphery of his vision, Beckett saw two of the Tepes clan fall under the onslaught of glinting blades, but he couldn't take his eyes away from the fat, blood-engorged Tepes that was bearing down on him. He began to pray to the God of his abandonment as he began to accept the fact that they were going to be slaughtered.

If that was the case, he was going to take Vasile Tepes along with him. Once he could get to him, that was.

A dark shadow appeared behind him and Beckett feared that this was the end – one in front and one behind him did not bode well. His mind fleetingly dwelt on which one would kill him. Irrelevant. He was about to die.

The blade from behind swished through the air and made contact with the fat, blood-gorged Tepes in the abdomen, and then, thrust upwards hard behind the ribs, slicing through lung tissue and piercing the heart. It was withdrawn with a loud sucking sound and swung again as Alexis Vasilakis took off the head.

Beckett swung around, momentarily confused that he was still alive. Then he heard Mihai's voice, "Alexis! Good timing!" was all he could process and say as another Tepes threw himself forwards.

Darius was deep in a torrent of blood-lust, partly fuelled by his hunger and partly by a rage that he had thought he had forgotten in his search for his brother, Andrei. Years had passed in the care of Beckett and Lane, and the lust for revenge had died along with his brother, but, at that moment, in that split-second in time, his eyes lighted on Constantin Tepes.

Images of the Sanctuary on fire, the knowledge of the dying client that he couldn't reach, the exquisite pain of the turning, the evil in the blood that had turned him, all surged into a whirlpool of pure hatred that was never going to be contained.

Constantin saw him at the same time and flew towards him, blade raised. Steel clashed and both blades clattered to the floor. It was one-on-one now. Darius's hands were around Constantin's throat, his canines down and dripping with blood from his last encounter, the blood vessels in his eyes turning the whites crimson. He was snarling and saliva foamed at the side of his mouth, as the rest of the blood-letting and chaos retreated and it was just the two of them.

Blood spurted, as arteries opened and then began to close again. Animal noises that originated from the hellish confines of dark souls took over, and suddenly, they were rolling on the floor each trying to get their teeth into the other's throat.

A cry of triumph ripped through the air and, in that moment, they both became still as the snow beneath their entwined bodies turned into a spreading red stain. Neither of them moved.

Beckett saw it and let out a cry from the depths of his despair, "Noooooo!" He turned towards Darius but was pulled back in another onslaught from yet another Tepes.

Seconds expanded into minutes and then Darius rolled off the inert body of Constantin Tepes. His face was covered in gore as he had bitten through Constantin's carotid artery and drained him of all that he could swallow. His face was a red mess. His eyes were black and bloody. His chest was heaving and he lowered his head to regain his composure.

It was enough. Radu saw his moment. His revenge on Andrei Tepes would have to be transferred to the brother.

He would have his revenge by proxy.

As he walked slowly and deliberately towards Darius, everything seemed surreal. This was his moment.

He caught hold of Darius's jacket and spun him around. "This is for my mother, who was slaughtered in her bed by your brother."

He raised the stake and homed in on the place on Darius's chest that would take the stake between his ribs and into his heart. Maybe he would sleep at night again. The stake had begun its arc of descent.

"I don't think so, you bastard!"

Mike took Radu's head clean off his shoulders and kicked it away with a bloodied boot. Darius stood upright and stared at him. "Thanks," he said, as he spat some of Constantin's flesh onto the red snow.

"I owed you," Mike said, his breath coming in violent heaves.

CHAPTER THIRTY-SEVEN: STARING INTO THE ABYSS

In the heart of the red mist, Beckett cast a rapid glance around and saw that not only had they survived, but Tepes blood had been spilled in bucket loads and the snow was awash with it. The others had decided that perhaps the House of Tepes would survive better if more of its members remained alive; they had vanished among the ruins and were, by now, heading back down to the valley below.

There was a silence that claimed all, and for a moment they paused to take stock.

Lane was bleeding from a gash across her arm and one on her face, but both had begun to heal. Beckett was breathless and his rage was still unspent. Mike stood next to him, ready to defend his friend against another onslaught.

Two bodies lay among the Tepes dead: Lafayette and Jean-Baptiste. Lane was on her knees leaning over the First One, and, as she turned his head towards her and it rolled onto her own knee, she allowed herself a small cry of anguish, but quickly realised that there was more going on than would allow for her despair.

Lafayette lay in a spreading red pool and lifted his arm towards her, and she moved to his side in an instant, unable to do anything now for Jean-Baptiste. She cradled his head on her bloodied knee and wiped his blood away from his eyes. The wound in his chest was bad, but perhaps not mortal. It would depend onhow quickly they could get him to a place of safety to allow him into the Long Sleep. It didn't look good. She looked across at Mihai and shook her head.

Mihai made a step towards her and began to speak – words that ended in a strangled gurgling sound, as Vasile thrust his blade with accomplished accuracy under Mihai's ribs from behind, his face a twisted mask of hatred. Lane's tears flooded her eyes and ran in rivulets down her cheeks as she saw her oldest friend cut down.

Vasile Tepes stood among the Tepes dead, his eyes black and empty as he began to call down Shemsu once more.

"No you don't," Mike snapped, and made a move towards him. An arm shot across his chest.

"Mine," was all Beckett said.

The stench of blood filled his nose and the sounds of the dead and dying re-played on an endless loop inside his head, mingling with the sound of Lane's sobs, but, above all that, the absolute dire need to end the life of Vasile Tepes became more vital than breathing. He pulled himself upright and stared into the abyss of Vasile's eyes, frozen in the moment and then, before his heart could beat again, Vasile was leaping towards him.

He crashed into Beckett, the force of which threw him back against the castle wall, knocking the wind from him and creating a pain in the middle of his back like nothing he had felt before. Vasile's eyes were full of death and his fury was written on every pore.

Beckett was acutely aware of the sheer drop that was onely a foot behind him and Vasile was taking full advantage, lifting Beckett off his feet and pushing him backwards. Beckett pushed back and for a moment it seemed as though his strength was no match for the blood-enraged Vasile. He was off his feet and Vasile could see victory only one thrust away. Then Beckett made a grab at Vasile and jumped onto the wall – if he was going over, he was going to take the Tepes bastard with him. Lane's gasp sounded like a supersonic boom in the tension that hung in the layered air.

By some miracle or unseen force, they both kept their

feet as Vasile realised his own mistake and pushed Beckett backwards away from the wall, jumping down after him, snarling like a rabid dog and seeking Beckett's throat. Blood and spittle flew as they tangled together mid-air, Beckett's face unrecognisable in the heat of the blood-rage. Lane drew a sharp breath; this was Beckett as she had never seen him and he terrified her.

Bestial snarls came from both of them as they fought to the death. Not one of the others dared move to assist Beckett, knowing instinctively that to interfere was to cause him to falter and lose the fight. They could only watch and pray.

Suddenly on their feet again, Beckett pushed Vasile away from him, the upper hand within his reach, but in some perverse universe he decided to make it last. Vasile, sensing defeat, backed away until the only place left him was the ancient crumbling wall again. He jumped onto it, the height giving him back the advantage. But Beckett launched himself into the attack again and was facing him on the wall once more.

Lane felt her heart miss its beat and her breathing stopped.

"Fuck this," Darius spat, as he bent to pick up one of the fallen blades and threw it into Beckett's waiting grip. As the blade sliced through flesh and sinew above Vasile's shoulders, his head appeared to wobble, just for a millisecond, and then he was gone, toppling off the wall, down the mountain, bouncing off the jagged rocks until he hit bottom.

Beckett allowed his head to drop as he stepped down from the ruined wall. The adrenaline and rage met exhaustion head-on and he felt his knees buckle and take him to the floor. Lane had him in her arms before any of the others moved.

Mike looked around at the bloody snow and the dead from both sides. The tell-tale muscle in his cheek twitched as he ground his teeth together. Enough was enough and in his opinion that line had been well and truly crossed. He bent to pick up one of the discarded blades.

In that moment the flames on the torches flared into the night sky as Vlad rose to his feet, desiccated no longer.

"You're fucking kidding me," Mike said, swinging the blade high.

Before it could reach the top of the arc, a booming noise and a great rush of air seemed to consume all breathable oxygen, as the Blood God, summoned repeatedly, materialised in front of them.

Shemsu appeared in his natural form; an enormous, muscle-bound man's body clothed only in the pleated linen kilt of the pharaohs and with the head of a lion. In his hand was a wine-press.

Once summoned, Shemsu demanded a blood sacrifice and he made his choice …

CHAPTER THIRTY-EIGHT: THE BLOOD GOD

No blade was required. Shemsu's hand reached out, displaying the talons at the end of huge fingers that reached out and ripped Vlad's body in two. The ancient Prince's face was still set in an expression of victory that had no time to transpire.

No-one moved as Shemsu fell on his prey and began to devour him; they couldn't, they were paralysed – the presence of the Blood God had its own dark magic.

His lion's jaws tore the flesh from Vlad's bones and the sound of crunching bone hung in the air until he tossed aside the remains of his kill. He picked up Vlad's head and with one deft movement he tossed it into the wine-press and promptly de-materialised.

Mike knew a demon when he saw one – that was his territory – but he refrained from comment. What would be the point, it had gone back to its own hell?

Several minutes elapsed as they all sought to bring the reality of their situation into focus.

There had been terrible losses – Mihai and Jean-Baptiste – and there was still the possibility of losing Lafayette. Lane seemed inconsolable and Beckett had no clue how to comfort her. Mihai would always be that spectre between them now. They hadn't been involved romantically, as far as he knew, but she had always turned to Mihai when the chips were down and he knew that there was love between them. He wondered if he'd done enough to fill that role from then on. Somehow he doubted it.

Alexis Vasilakis went to Beckett and Lane. "I am so sorry for the loss of the Patriarch," he said.

It was Beckett that replied. "I wasn't sure which side you'd taken. I always thought the House of Vasilakis stood with Vasile."

Alexis seemed to ponder the comment. "Perhaps, at one time, but the raw truth of it was that the House of Tepes was set to rule us all – the Council would be extinguished along with the Created and the last of the vampire wars would eventually bring about the destruction of our race – I saw no sense in that. And I had my own score to settle with Vasile; he badly mistreated someone I care for."

Lane raised an eyebrow.

"Davina Marinescu." He met Darius's gaze. "She's your cousin, Darius – another victim of your brother's unquenchable thirst. I met her at Vasile's home. He left her for dead when his obsession for another took hold of him. Luckily, her grandfather, Nicolae, brought her to me. She is at present in the Long Sleep, healing. You will find Nicolae's body out there in the snow; his heart gave out I'm afraid. But at least he didn't die bloody."

He looked around – now the oldest of the vampires present, older than Lane by a century – and continued. "The Council must carry on and I have a letter from Mihai, signed and endorsed by the rest of the Curia. We have no Patriarch now, instead we have a Matriarch. Serve us well, Lane. You have the support of the most important of the vampire Houses. It will be a long time before the name of Tepes engenders fear again, and in that time we hope that sense will prevail among those who supported them."

"I don't know what to say," Lane managed. "Are you saying that Mihai knew that he was going to die here?"

Alexis shrugged, "Let's just say he was being cautious. A power vacuum is no good for any of us. You should call an emergency meeting of the Council; there is much to settle."

He took his leave and said in parting, "Drop the bodies

over the wall into the valley; the snow will cover them and no-one will be up here again before the spring. I still have some influence with the more rational of our kind in this region and I will arrange for no trace to be left here. These ruins will stay ruined and remain nothing more than a tourist attraction, and the name Vlad Dracula will be consigned back to history and fiction."

And he was gone.

Beckett saw his plans for his future with Lane, the Matriarch of the Council, begin to fade. She read him.

"I'm still me. I still intend to rebuild the Sanctuary and make sure the others are too, in every city. It means I won't have time for my clinical practice, it's yours now – yours and Darius's. And if you think you can walk away from me, you're wrong. You're Beckett, my vampire priest who will always be there to hear my confession. Good enough?"

He allowed his face to try and smile, "Good enough. We need to move quickly now, we need to get Lafayette to safety, so let's start shoving this lot over the edge. And there's something else." He nodded towards the hearth where the Bloody Chalice lay in a wide red pool of Tepes blood. "We have to deal with that; it needs to never see the light of day again."

"I'll take it," Mike said.

CHAPTER THIRTY-NINE: LOCKED AWAY

Roman Wolfe leaned on his desk, his fingers steepled under his chin as he listened to Mike's account.

"I don't say that it is the last of the conflict between the Born and the Created – there are others like Vasile Tepes out there. But for now …"

"So, what is it that you're not telling me?" Roman asked.

Mike stood up and left the room. When he returned he had a small holdall with him, which he placed on the desk.

"This needs … safe keeping," he said. "I don't recommend you touch it." He unzipped the hold-all and opened it wide.

Roman bent over it. "The chalice. Well, we have just about the safest place for it. Let's do it now."

Mike picked up the holdall and together they descended to the basement levels, Roman opening all of the doors with his retinal scans and hand-prints. As they walked through the armoury, and the room containing sacred objects and power amulets, neither of them spoke. At the far end, Roman activated the scanner that gave them entry into a long room with artefacts in lead-lined cases. This was where the objects that had evil connotations and were deemed dangerous were locked away from the world, and this was to be the secure home of the Bloody Chalice.

Roman used his hand-print to open an empty, lead-lined case and Mike placed the chalice inside without a word. He nodded his satisfaction as he heard the security bolts fall into place in the box.

His first act on returning to the Strazca headquarters

had been to run up the curved staircase and into his wife's room. Beth greeted him as if he had been away for an hour or so, with her usual faraway smile. He hugged her tightly and was suddenly and strangely glad that she was locked in this world of hers, away from vampires and their wars, away from demons and things that had no right to be in this world. In her world it was always sunshine and the occasional rose. His was in a stark contrast.

Now, with the chalice secure, he had returned to her side.

He sensed a presence behind him and Beckett stood framed in the doorway.

"How is she?" he asked, in doctor mode.

"Same as always," Mike said, as he turned away lest Beckett see the tear forming in his eye. "She's happy."

Beckett said nothing as he sat in the comfortable armchair opposite Mike and Beth on the sofa. There wasn't any need for words for them both to feel the strengthened bond between them that was now far beyond simple friendship.

"How's Darius?" Mike asked.

"Hungry."

Mike couldn't prevent the involuntary laugh that escaped him. "He's always going to be hungry, that one."

Beckett smiled. "It will get less. But Roman has kindly said we can stay here while we rebuild the Sanctuary and make use of these facilities. Darius has a room on the floor above this one and Raven is determined to be his donor. We have time to gather blood from other resources too, so … Darius is going to be OK."

"And Lafayette?"

"Lane has used our network resources to fly him back to New Orleans. Apparently there is a woman there named Monique, lives out on the bayou. Don't know how she knew what had happened to Lafayette but she made contact with Lane somehow and demanded he be brought to her to 'recover'. That was the word she used, but it seemed to contain an unspoken understanding of his condition. She said something about 'the bones'. He was in and out of early Long Sleep and seemed happy with that arrangement and asked Lane to make sure there was a bottle of good rum for the woman." He shrugged, "I don't know, Mike, but if she'll care for him, that's all we can ask."

"It's all any of us can ask," Mike said gently. "So, what now for you?"

Beckett leaned back against the comfortable sofa. "For now, I'm going to look after Darius's full transition, and oversee the re-build of the Sanctuary, long-distance. I can keep an eye on Beth, too. At some point I'll go back to the practice in Abergavenny, but not yet. In the meantime … in the meantime I have to stake my claim somewhere else." He grinned.

Mike grinned back. "Lane?"

"Lane," Beckett said.

"And Helena? Is there any progress?"

"Some," Beckett replied. "At least now they know it's genetic; once they find the correct genome to silence they are almost there. But Helena has a problem. An ethical one."

Mike frowned. "How so?"

"It's a matter of 'Disease or Species'. Put quite simply: if they succeed, is it ethical to silence the gene in the Born, because their vampirism is in their nature; they are a species. The Created have been infected, essentially, and their natural DNA altered, so … a disease. Once she gets her head around it the rest will follow."

"There's a load for all of us to get our heads around," Mike said in a lowered tone. "But we will, because we have to."

THANK YOU!

To my Reader:

Many thanks for buying *Sanctuary*, I hope you enjoyed reading it.

If you did enjoy it, please post a review at Amazon, Goodreads or your favourite social network site and let your friends know about *Sanctuary*.

I hope that this has whetted your appetite to read my other novels. You can find details of these in the next page as well as the short stories collections.

And don't forget to sign up for my newsletter for details of my latest books and a FREE short story at:

janmcdonaldemailsign-up.gr8.com

Happy Reading!
All the best
Jan

ALSO BY JAN MCDONALD

Mike Travis Paranormal Investigations
The Crowsmoor Curse: getBook.at/Crowsmoorcurse

Long Shadows: getBook.at/longshadows

The Sacred Ark: getBook.at/sacredark

The Haunted Diary of Victoria Little:
getBook.at/haunteddiary

The Merlin Manuscript: getBook.at/merlin

The Sin Eater: getbook.at/sineater

Mike Travis Demon Hunter
Fallen Angels and Demons: getBook.at/FallenAngels

The Demon Ark: getBook.at/DemonArk

Mike Travis short stories
Beginnings: getBook.at/Beginnings

Halloween: getBook.at/halloween

Christmas Spirits: getBook.at/christmasspirits

The Beckett Vampire Trilogy
Midnight Wine: getBook.at/midnightwine

Lycan: getBook.at/lycan

ABOUT JAN MCDONALD

Jan lives close to the Welsh borders which have their own mystical quality and provide endless resources in the way of legends and folklore surrounding paranormal experiences. She loves all things paranormal and has read the best: Dennis Wheatley, Stephen King, Edgar Allan Poe, Bram Stoker and all those authors that excel in the creepy or downright scary world of paranormal events.

When she embarked on the Mike Travis series, she realised that the field of paranormal investigation is more than we see on the popular TV programmes. So in order to provide compelling ghost hunting tales but with the greatest accuracy, Jan trained as a Paranormal Investigator and has studied parapsychology.

CONTACT DETAILS

Visit the authors website:
jan-mcdonald.co.uk

Follow on Twitter:
www.twitter.com/janmcdonald1

Cover designed by: www.stunningbookcovers.com
Cover art: © theartofphoto - Fotolia.com

Published by: Raven Crest Books
www.ravencrestbooks.com

Like us on Facebook:
Facebook.com/ravencrestbooksclub

Printed in Great Britain
by Amazon

54702723R00129